His Lies, Her Secrets

Christine E.M. Cooper

Prologue

Her eyes locked with mine as she pointed the heavy piece of metal at me. In that moment I not only wondered who she was but what I had done to her for her to want to kill me. My mind was racing and there were a million thoughts running through my head. With my hands in the air, I could feel sweat dripping from places that I didn't even know existed. The knots in my stomach were getting tighter by the second and I was beginning to feel light-headed. To say that I was terrified would have been an understatement. I was face-to-face with the barrel of some random woman's three-eighty and I had no idea why. I didn't know what had brought her to my hotel room at this hour. I racked my brain trying to remember her face but to no avail.

She was a beautiful woman and I was certain that I wouldn't have forgotten a face like hers. It was hard to imagine her in a setting other than the one where she threatened to blow a hole through my exposed chest. I couldn't stop shaking as I prayed that this was just a nightmare. She looked like someone from my most erotic dreams.

I scrutinized her face and started to feel like I had seen her before. Her golden skin shone so bright in the dim light that it seemed to light up the once dark space around her. This woman had it going on. Her high cheek bones perfectly complimented the sexiest pair of lips that I had ever seen and I couldn't help but notice her beautiful eyes. From where I sat on the floor, they appeared to be a bright green color. I figured they had to be contacts since her skin was darker than mine. She wore them well and pulled them off better than most, without a doubt. This woman looked like she belonged on the cover of Vogue magazine. It would have been hard to have forgotten a face and body like the one she had if we had previously crossed paths. Hell, if I wasn't about to be murdered by the psychotic bitch, I would have been trying to get with her. I tried hard for the next few minutes to remember the familiar stranger but I just couldn't put my finger on exactly how it was that I knew this woman.

I still didn't know her reason for being in my hotel room at ten o'clock at night so I offered to let her take anything she wanted. I even assured her that I wouldn't inform the authorities that she was ever here. The fact that my wife was a top notch detective made that statement a lie for sure but I was willing to say and do anything at that point for her to get the hell out of my room. I was helpless and she had all the power. All I had were my words. I started offering her deals on attorney fees should she ever need help beating a case in the future. I even started naming the occupations of my friends and offering out their services free of charge. By the time I was done begging for her to spare my life, I had set her up with a lifetime worth of free catering, carpet cleanings and mechanic services. I could tell that she wasn't buying any of it. Out of nowhere, I started to shiver uncontrollably.

The room was cold and I was in nothing but my underwear. She started laughing as if she was getting some kind of sick pleasure out of watching me suffer. I was so close to shitting myself and I wondered for a second if that would have brought her satisfaction. When the laughter stopped, she smiled mischievously.

I didn't know what she was planning to do next. She started walking around me in slow steps, sizing me up and slowly shaking her head. She began teasing me by pointing the gun at different parts of my body. I jumped when she pressed the gun against my chest and slid it down slowly. She chuckled which let me know that the purpose was to get a reaction out of me. I was trying hard to keep myself together at that point. My breathing became heavier as I considered the possibility that I may be leaving this room in a body bag. Once she reached my lower abdomen, she pulled the gun away from me. Just as I was breathing for the first time in what felt like minutes, she aimed the three-eighty at my manhood. At that point, I lost it. "Please," I cried out. "Please don't do this." I begged with one hand in the air and the other cuffed tightly around my family jewels. The sick smile she wore earlier had turned into a frown. She stared me in the face as she removed the safety from the three-eighty that she had been gripping tightly in the palm of her hand for the past ten minutes.

I began praying like I had never prayed before. I made promises to get back into church and even visit relatives more often. I even made a commitment to volunteer at the homeless shelter on holidays, which is something my wife always begged me to do. I couldn't remember the last time I had made that many promises to the man upstairs. It's usually a last resort for me since I always found myself repeating the same sins that I had promised to turn away from. I was sure, though, that with God being a man he would definitely have understood where I was coming from. My balls and I were staring into the face of death and I wasn't sure how we were going to escape this one. I could hear over my cries the sound as she released one bullet into the chamber. I squeezed my eyes together tightly and prepared for the sound of the blast. With one motion, she pulled the trigger and it was all over.

Contents

ONE – BRYSON

As I pressed those seven numbers, I dreaded telling her that I wasn't going to make it tonight. Even though it was the norm for me, she still went ballistic every time I called with an excuse for not being able to make it to one of her events. It was her thirty-ninth birthday and here I was cancelling on her again. I felt a tremendous amount of guilt for doing what I was about to do. Hell, I felt like the worst person in the world for being so selfish. I knew what this party meant to her just like I knew what all the other events in the past meant. However, guilt or thoughts of my wife crying her eyes out tonight wasn't enough to make me want to hang up the phone. Hanging up would only mean that I'd be dialing a different number to do the exact same thing but with bigger consequences. Only a fool would play the game that way. There were rules that had to be followed and if they were ever broken I would be the biggest loser. You see, whether I'd like to admit it or not, I am caught in the middle of a love triangle that involves me, my wife and the woman that I am in love with.

My wife is beautiful, smart and everything I've ever wanted in a woman. I can honestly say that she is the best thing that has ever happened to me. People looking in from the outside often tell us that we have the perfect marriage. After two kids, she still managed to keep herself looking as good as the day we met, if not better. Married life had never given me any reason to complain. Of course sex had become almost nonexistent over the years, as in most marriages. After I started complaining about not getting any as often as I used to, she began telling me about something she had seen on Oprah. Some so called expert had said that the average married couple only had sex once a week. After hearing that, she had convinced herself that giving it up twice a week and on holidays was actually more than enough to keep me satisfied. Compared to our previous two to three times a day, whenever and wherever sex life, once or twice a week was a big change. Even with these crazy beliefs, I still only had eyes for my wife. The lack of sex didn't change things for me. I had gotten used to it as well as picking up my monthly supply of porn flicks from a bootlegger by the name of Meat Meat that my man Kyle had introduced me to.

Watching porn had become a ritual for me any time my wife and kids would leave me alone in the house. I would be like a child at Christmas whenever the door would close and Peyton and the kids would be off for the day. I can remember a time when I thought I had heard her car pull out of the driveway one Saturday morning. She had given me confirmation that they would only be gone for a couple of hours as well as a list of things to do around the house while they were out. After calculating in my head the time it would take for me to get everything done, I knew that I wouldn't have much time for myself. Once I heard her accelerate, I jumped off the couch that I had appeared so comfortable on just seconds prior and raced to the bedroom. I ran my hand under the mattress in an attempt to grab any one of the DVDs that I had purchased the day before. I read the front of the CD where Meat Meat had scribbled the title with a black sharpie, "Chocolate Candy Drops". After ripping it out of the paper I dashed over to the DVD player and inserted it. Immediately, two sistas that looked to be in their mid to late twenties popped up on the screen. They were fine as hell with their smooth dark skin and long black hair. They were walking towards the screen as if they were coming to give me the fantasy of a lifetime.

As I got lost in the moment, the camera turned towards the lucky guy who was about to engage in one good fuck. He sat there grinning like a Cheshire cat stroking his dick, preparing himself for the moment. As one of the women wasted no time bending down in front of him, the other grabbed her partner's hair so that the camera could get a clear shot of the professional blow job Mr. Lucky was now getting. She bobbed up and down his shaft and sucked as if her life depended on it. On the other side of the screen I began massaging my own dick while pretending that I was a part of the action. I concentrated on the scene in front of me because I was interested in what Miss Hair Holder's roll in all of this was going to be. After satisfaction appeared on his face, Mr. Lucky flipped the woman who had just been pleasing him onto her back and began eating her out.

I was enjoying the moment when all of a sudden he signaled for the second woman to join them. She stood patiently with her index finger in her mouth. When she began sucking her partner's plump breasts, I almost lost it. I stroked myself harder but stopped each time I felt myself getting close to the big bang. I wasn't ready to climax just yet. It had been a couple of weeks since I had the opportunity to be alone. Between Peyton's monthly visit from "Aunt Flow" and her just not being in the mood after long days at work, I was officially sex deprived. I was horny as hell and I wanted to hold onto this moment for as long as possible.

About five minutes into the DVD I heard a soft voice call from what sounded like the living room. "Daddy," she said over and over again. In a panic, I quickly scrambled to pull up my boxers before jumping out of the bed. "I'm coming sweetheart," I managed to say in a voice as calm as I could muster, considering the circumstances. I reached over and grabbed my jogging pants from the floor and stumbled to her rescue. "What is it sweetheart?" I found her standing at the door smiling. "Mommy wants you to come look at her wheel. She ran over a bottle and said a very bad word." As I walked outside to my family's rescue, now feeling somewhat normal, I saw a smirk on my wife's face. I could tell that she was aware of what I had been engaged in. Her face told me that she received an excessive amount of pleasure from sending our daughter inside to interrupt me.

As I walked toward the car, she held back laughter by covering her mouth and all I could do was roll my eyes and shake my head. We said nothing while staring at each other before bursting into laughter. I checked out the tire, let her and my baby girl know that everything was fine and I reached over and gave my son a pound. As I looked back at her on my way into the house, she cleared her throat to get my attention. "I was planning to give you some tonight but I guess you already have that taken care of," she chuckled. I smiled at her and pretended to not be in a hurry to make my way back to the place where it was all about to pop off.

This day was like many days in my past, until my lover came along. I never knew what I was missing until I met her. She made me realize what had been lacking in my marriage. Her presence filled a void that I never knew existed. In fact, before her unexpected entrance into my life, I was never the type that would step outside of my marriage.

Hell, the thought never even crossed my mind. I had no intentions of breaking the vows my wife and I had made eighteen years prior, in front of God, our minister and a congregation full of our family and friends. I don't mean to go against the old cliché "it takes two to tango" but I was just minding my own business when she approached me.

"You look like you could use a hand with that?" I turned away from the mess that I had just made to find the most beautiful pair of legs known to mankind. As I sized her up, I also determined that she had to spend most of her days at the gym. "Damn," I thought to myself. "Who the hell is this?" After slowly getting up from the floor, I found myself face-to-face with her. She was gorgeous and she had a smell to match. "Uh hello, you must be Jackie's replacement," I said while extending my hand towards her. "That would be me," she said as she held my hand in a way that said more than just 'it's nice to meet you'. It was more like 'voulez vous coucher avec moi'.

While she stared at me, I had the pleasure of looking into her mysterious dark brown eyes. They sparkled from the light that bounced off of the glass counter tops that I personally picked out for the lobby. I wasn't sure if it was her eyes or the way that her thick dark hair sat perfectly on her shoulders. One of the two made her so appealing to me. I also couldn't help but notice her flawless skin complexion. The woman looked as though she bathed in butter every night. "So, is that a yes?" She stared at me with her perfectly arched eyebrows raised while she waited for my response. "Yes, please. I would appreciate that very much," I said as I released her hand. She helped me gather the straws, chopsticks, paper cups and lids from the floor. I took the opportunity to steal another glance. Her beauty had caught me off guard. "Chinese huh?" she asked. "Yeah, all of this is the result of a bet," I told her. "I lost and now I get to buy lunch for fifteen every Friday for a month. Lucky for you this is only the first Friday." The fact that I found it completely impossible to take my eyes off of her caught me by surprise. "Yes, lucky for me," she responded. "And lucky for you, I'll be here to help you retrieve it all from your car next time." I chuckled at her sarcasm as I gathered the heavy brown paper bags that smelled strongly of beef and broccoli, shrimp fried rice and a number of other goodies I picked up from A Taste of China. Meanwhile, she grabbed the jug of tea and paper products and followed me to the break room. "Thank you," I said to my new assistant. "No problem. The pleasure was all mine." She smiled seductively, flashing a set of teeth so white that I was blinded by the sight.

The thoughts that filled my head as I watched her leave the break room continued to catch me off guard. I felt guilty imagining myself doing things to her that I had until now, only imagined myself doing to my wife. No other woman had ever made me feel this way before and I knew at that moment that having this woman by my side every single day as my assistant would soon be one of my most difficult challenges.

TWO – PEYTON

"Bryson Jr," I called upstairs to my son for the third time. "Is there a reason why you're not at least dressed and it's past seven o'clock?" I asked after my second born finally appeared in the doorway of the kitchen. "Mom, it's senior cut day," he answered sleepily. "And?" I paused. "You're not a senior". He looked perplexed. "Mom, I can't believe you're trippin like this. I will be the only person sitting in a class all day by myself. Everybody's cutting today. There won't be anybody there but me and the principal. Even the teachers are calling out today." I traded my 'who are you talking to with that slang' look in for a simple shake of my head. "B.J., just go back to bed, but-," I paused. "I better not have to find you today. If I call that phone, you better answer or I will find you." I stared at him for a minute just to make sure I had his full attention. Don't forget your mama's a P.I. I can locate you in less than fifteen minutes if I need to."

After putting fear into him, he leaned over and kissed me on the cheek. I still couldn't believe how tall he was at fifteen. It seemed like just the other day I was buying him superhero underwear and now he towers over me. "Love you ma," he said. "Yeah, I love you too," I replied. "Make sure you tell Jessica to call me when she wakes up," I commanded. "Ma, you might be better off telling sleeping beauty what you need to tell her later tonight cause I guarantee you she'll be in bed at least until then," he joked. As I turned to walk out the door he called out to me. "Oh and by the way mom, happy birthday." I smiled as I made eye contact with my youngest child. "Uh huh, you thought I forgot didn't you?" he joked. "Thank you baby," I said trying my best to conceal my emotions. So far, he was the first person to tell me happy birthday and I actually thought that he'd forgotten.

On my way to work I decided to call my husband to see if he had made it to his destination safely. I also wanted to see how his conference was going. "Hello," he answered. "Hey babe. How's everything going?" I got straight to point. He had informed me years ago that his time on the phone during conferences would be limited. He let me know early on that he would only have enough time for a quick chat before he would have to end the call. He explained how his colleagues would tap on their watches every other second that he'd have the phone up to his ear. While I learned to respect that, I still didn't like it. "So far, so good. And you?" he asked. "Same here. Apparently today's senior cut day and not only is Jessica staying home but so is B.J." I thought this would have sent him into a string of questions, such as; why I allowed him to stay home or why I spoil him so much.

He came from an old school home where there were fewer privileges. He was blown away when I told him about a few of the times I cut school back in the day. Cutting school was not an option for him. His parents believed that if the school doors were open, he and his siblings better had been there. Instead of questioning me about my decision to allow our son to participate in senior cut day, he showed no concern at all. In fact, all I got was the closing of the call.

"Well, thanks for calling. I'll talk to you later," he said before abruptly hanging up. "Well, goodbye to you too," I replied to no one at all.

"Good Morning Peyton. Chester was kind enough to bring in a hot box of fresh glazed arm and thigh plumpers. This is just what I needed right before our family portraits that are scheduled for next weekend. If you want some they're in the conference room." My colleague and good friend offered shortly after I arrived at work. "Thanks for the heads up Gloria. I'll do my best to go nowhere near there because I know that if I catch the slightest bit of aroma, it's over for me," I responded with a chuckle. "I don't know if you want to miss these. He must've caught the hot sign on because they are definitely fresh and well worth the calories," she informed me in that northern accent that I loved hearing so much.

Once I arrived in my office I quickly noticed the bright red flashing light on my phone, alerting me that someone had called and left me a message. Since it was first thing in the morning, this could only mean that this caller either called late yesterday or early this morning. I was slightly curious as to what this caller needed.

I picked up the receiver and entered the password to access my voicemail. "You have one new message. To listen to your messages, press one." Just as the caller was about to speak, there was a knock at my office door. I motioned for my visitor to enter. "Detective Hainesworth, I was wondering if you wanted a donut before Peter demolishes the last two," said the annoying intern. "No thanks, Cindy. I'm fine," I said with the phone's receiver resting on my shoulder and my index finger hovering over the dial pad. I was hoping that she would get the hint and do an about face out of my office. "Well, we would really like for you to have at least one. I mean, you look great to be almost forty. There's really no need to be watching your figure day in and day out." I gave the skinny twenty-two-year old a look that indicated I didn't appreciate her unsolicited advice.

At this point, I knew exactly what was going on. They sent Cindy to lure me into the conference room for a surprise of some sort for my birthday. This was typical of them. Every year, they would get together and plan a little party for me. Either that or they would treat me to lunch and have some unenthusiastic waiter come out with a cake and sing a monotone rendition of happy birthday.

Before I went over to the conference room to allow my colleagues to try and surprise me with the balloons, cake and whatever else they usually used for work celebrations, I decided to satisfy my curiosity and check the message I had attempted to check before. I listened with my pen in hand as the woman's voice flowed through the speakers. "Hello," she paused. "I received your phone number from a friend who has used your services and I was hoping that you could help me as well. Please give me a call back at 410-555-3324." After the message was complete, I hung up the phone. "Sweetheart this is not the guessing game." I tossed the phone number that I had just written down directly into file thirteen.

Although her not leaving me enough information was one of my pet peeves, I still found myself wondering who this woman was and exactly what it was that she needed my help with. She sounded as though her issue was not a very pressing one. Therefore, I wasn't in any hurry to call her back, especially since I had a very strict rule of not returning calls to those who didn't leave both their name and number.

THREE – BRYSON

After only the second week, my new assistant quickly became my motivation to go to work each day. "Would you have a problem staying overtime a couple nights a week if needed?" I asked her during one of our one-on-one training sessions. Jackie never had a problem with the extra required hours. During the times when she and I would stay and work late, she stayed in her office and I stayed in mine.

My new assistant was different. She was no Jackie. Jackie was fifty-seven, wrinkled and even had grandchildren. Her replacement, however, was twenty-three, smoother than a baby's ass and kid-free. "No, not at all," she answered. "I'm available any time you need me. I have absolutely nothing waiting at home for me but Sarge."

She stared at me with furrowed brows which matched the exact look on my face. "Oh, boyfriend, huh?" I was trying hard not to show too much concern and curiosity. I had already skimmed over her interview paperwork and learned that she had no children. "Well, he does keep me warm at night and kisses me goodbye each day before I leave my apartment. He also protects me. Oh, and he'll bite if you get too close to me," she paused. "Sarge is your dog,

11

isn't he?" I asked slightly embarrassed. She giggled before answering. "The most beautiful Rottweiler in the world." It was music to my ears hearing that she was not only single but that her availability was wide open. This confirmed that she could stay any time and for as long as I needed her to.

Things got a little heated during one of our long days at the office. "You about ready to wrap things up?" Without ever looking up from her computer, she answered. "I just need a couple more minutes to finish what I'm working on, then I'll be ready." She turned her head from side to side like she was trying to release stress from the long workday.

She snatched a huge pin out of her perfectly even jet-black hair with one quick motion and ran her fingers through it. I was caught in a trance watching her put on the seductive show that she didn't even know she was the star of. She shook her head and allowed her thick dark hair to sway from side to side, causing my mind to go places it shouldn't. I could feel the bulge in my pants grow as I watched her make herself more comfortable. I felt like I could've exploded when she removed her cardigan and began shifting her bra to ensure that her cleavage spilled out perfectly over her tight lace cami.

I was brought back to reality when she suddenly shot me a glance. "Is something wrong?" I cleared my throat while stalling to think of a reason for me to be standing in her doorway minutes after our conversation had ended. "No, nothing at all," I stumbled over my words. She had me feeling like I was a teenage boy who had just been caught peeping at girls in the locker room. "Just give me a ring when you get ready to shut down." I was embarrassed as hell. I got about halfway down the hall when I heard her call my name. "Bryce." I loved it when she called me by the name that only those close to me had. It made me feel like we had some kind of connection, one bigger than that of just employer and employee. I turned around and walked back towards her office. "Whoa." I stood in her doorway and stared at her nipples through her exposed fancy bra. When she was sure that she had my full attention, she dropped the skirt that I had been so jealous of all day long.

"Damn," I said as I thought about the moments when I had walked behind her during trips to and from the break room and meetings throughout the day. I so badly wanted to be the cloth that had the pleasure of rubbing up against her voluptuous hips and thighs. She started walking in my direction and my manhood reacted as she neared. I hadn't been with any other woman besides my wife since we had gotten married so the mere thought of her touching me made me tense up a bit. She came closer.

"What's the matter?" She rested her hands on my shoulders while she wasted no time introducing her lips to mine. I didn't say a word. I just stood there and allowed her to please me with her tongue. "You know you want it," she whispered in my ear. She began unbuttoning my shirt and even though I wanted to stop her, I couldn't. It was like I was experiencing an episode of Sleep Paralysis when you have one of those dreams and you feel like something has you pinned down. No matter what you do you can't be released. Even as you try to pull away you end up weak and limp because you have no control over your body. As a kid, my mother used to tell me that the devil was riding me because I had misbehaved that day. It's funny because if she had the slightest clue of what I was doing at that moment, that would be the very thing she would tell me.

Before I knew it, she had me on the floor of her office. She had already managed to get my shirt and slacks off. She began kissing me from top to bottom and I knew that there was no turning back. As she made her way down south, I had a pretty good assumption that this was going to be my lucky night. It had been so long since my wife had done such a favor for me. She would think of any and every excuse not to go down on me. Until now, I had just accepted the fact that I would never feel the sensation of a woman's mouth caressing my manhood. As she approached it, I wasn't sure if I wanted to shout or cry. Just as I had assumed, she worked her way down and went to work.

FOUR – BRYSON

My whole body relaxed as she sucked me in a way like no other woman had before. As she moaned I became hornier and more anxious to release inside of her mouth. I had only dreamed of this moment for years which is why it was so hard to hold back. I was trying with everything in me not to get mine. I started trying to think of things that would temporarily put me out of the mood like the Delaney Case that had been a pain in my ass for over a month now. That only worked for about a nanosecond.

She started sucking harder and slower as if she could read my mind. It's like she knew that it was exactly how I liked it. "Oh shit. Girl if you keep that up this will be the farthest we'll get." I struggled to speak, taking breaks between every couple of words. She must've taken me seriously because she slowly released my manhood from her mouth and kissed her way back up to my face.

Once she reached her destination, she positioned herself on top of me. Without wasting any time, she grabbed my rock hard manhood and slid it inside of her. Her moans began to fill the room and I took that as a compliment. This had to have meant that my size was to her liking. That didn't come as a surprise to me since every woman in my past had always praised me for being blessed in that department.

Her moans became louder as she slid up and down my soldier. This alone almost made me reach my peak, especially while watching her big round breasts bounce up and down. "Damn she had it going on," I thought. She then reached down and began playing with her clit. This woman was a freak. My wife had never been the type to please herself sexually, at least not while she knew I was watching. The few times we'd watch porn together in the past, she would become all sanctified whenever a woman would pop up on the screen playing with herself. I knew better though.

I had grown up as the only boy in a house full of sisters and I had learned more than I ever wanted to know about how the female mind worked. From my understanding, there wasn't a woman in this world who didn't know her body better than a man did. A female is known to find spots that a man could spend an eternity looking for and I wasn't about to be fooled by my wife and her holier than thou attitude.

All of a sudden, I felt her start to tighten and she began to slow up the pace a bit. "Oh shit, ooh," she moaned. With my hands still gripping her butt, I slowed down to allow her to gain her composure. "No, don't stop. Keep doing what you're doing. Please don't stop," she begged while her body began to jerk like it had been controlled by some powerful force that was bigger than her. I followed her commands and did as I was told. A few seconds later, it was my turn. "Oh shit, ah shit," I yelled as I pumped harder inside of her. Moments later we were both satisfied and contemplating round two.

The next day at work was a little awkward for me. We had fucked three times that night and I was unsure of what the morning after would be like. I arrived a few minutes early, as I always had. This was my time to have my coffee and catch up on the day's news. My phone rang shortly after getting settled. The caller ID informed me that it was my new assistant's extension. "This is Bryson," I answered nervously. I already knew what this was. This was going to be her telling me how much she regretted what happened last night and how she doesn't know what came over her. She was going to ask me if we could just forget about what happened between the two of us and if we could just have a business relationship from here on out all because she would be afraid of being portrayed as some type of easy freak.

"Good morning. I just wanted to let you know that I had a good time last night and-," she paused. "I hope the feelings are mutual." She said nothing as she waited for my response. I cleared my throat. "Well, I'd be lying if I said I didn't enjoy myself as well." I spoke quietly since my office door was slightly open. There was an awkward moment of silence and I could feel her smiling through the phone. "I guess I'd better be getting back to work now. I wouldn't want to upset my boss," she said jokingly. I laughed quietly before hanging up the phone.

It had been almost eleven years since I banged my assistant on the floor of her office. What started out as just two people satisfying each other's needs turned into more than I could've ever expected. I never planned to lead a double life which involves a separate home that I share with my eleven-year old son, Bryson Jr, and his mother. I had intended to have a good time but one thing lead to another.

Shortly after our first few sexual escapades, our sessions became those of love-making. We went from quickly getting dressed and rushing out of the office after sex to spending a few minutes spooning and discussing each other's lives and aspirations. This came as a surprise to me because I never realized how much I missed this with Peyton until I found it in the arms of another woman.

Shortly after my lover and I made sex a part of our everyday lives, we decided that our working relationship would sooner or later bring conflict to our love life. After only a month of working together, I made arrangements for her to quietly leave the firm. Fortunately, I was able to get her a gig at my partner's firm just up the block from where I was located.

While her leaving my firm was in our best interest, we had to accept that it would cancel out any opportunity we had for a few moments of intimacy throughout the workday. I knew immediately that I would miss the times when she would come to my office as soon as everyone had successfully left the building. Hell, most of the time I would already have my pants half way off the second I heard the guard's keys jingle. The sound of those doors locking was the best sound in the world to me. The sound alone made my manhood harden.

On one particular night she crawled into my office wearing nothing but her bra, matching panties and sexy knee high stockings. When she reached my desk, she hopped on top of it and proceeded to give me a strip show. She performed so well that I can remember wondering if she had prior experience in that area. After all, I had paid big money to see strippers that weren't nearly as talented as she was. That night after she was completely naked, she gave me the time of my life. It was that night when I decided that I didn't want to go another day without her having a more permanent position in my life and I was willing to do anything in my power to make that happen. We tried our best to keep things flowing smoothly.

She would even allow me to come over to her place during lunch breaks. During desperate times, we would use the backseat of my Escalade. This was something I hadn't done since my senior year of high school. This was all new to me since spontaneity didn't exist with Peyton. She was a good girl who strongly felt like love making was meant for the bedroom only. I would often tell her that there was nothing wrong with a little freakiness whenever we had the urge, whether we were alone at home or in public.

After about six months into our relationship she started complaining about how we never go out. She even started throwing hints about a more serious commitment and even marriage. I gave her some sorry excuse about how I had been married before and I wasn't trying to go down that road again any time soon. Surprisingly, she bought it, but that wouldn't last for long. As for us never going out, I tried to make things right by taking her into towns outside of the one we lived in. I couldn't risk being seen with someone other than my wife. The last thing I wanted to do was complicate things at home. I had been lucky enough these past few years and that is the exact way I wanted to keep it. In fact, if you let my wife tell it, our eighteen-year marriage is indeed a happy one and it couldn't be better.

FIVE – VICTOR

"Get the fuck out of the way!" I sped around the no driving asshole that was in front of me. Once I got close enough, I rolled down my window. "Old ass should be at home knitting socks or some shit any damn way!" I sped off. It had been a long day and I was over the idiots in traffic who always seemed to drive cars that were too big for them to handle. All I wanted was to get home and see what the hell my wife had done all day. Just the thought of her sitting on her lazy ass made me clench my fists and grind my teeth.

After a long day at work I looked forward to releasing my anger out on her. She made it easy to do. Sometimes as soon as I walked in the door I would start in on what she did or didn't do and jump right into her punishment. She knew the exact way that I wanted things but she would often try me and that would result in consequences.

Tonight when I pulled up in the driveway, I noticed immediately that the house was dark. This wasn't like my wife to not be home this time of night, especially when she knew I was on my way home. She knew better than this shit. I pressed the remote to open up the garage door and proceeded to park my car. I couldn't wait to get in the house and call her up to see where the hell she was this time of night. She knew she was supposed to have her ass in this house by the time I got home every day or there would definitely be hell to pay when she got back. "I know this bitch must've really lost her damn mind". I grabbed my cell phone from the clip on my waist and dialed her number. She had some real explaining to do and I was ready to hear it. Even though nothing she had to say would matter at this point. The only thing that would get her out of this one was if somebody had died, nothing else mattered.

I turned my Bluetooth so that it pointed towards my mouth while positioning myself over the toilet to take a piss. I waited impatiently for her voice to come through the phone. "What the hell?" I noticed a note that was taped to the bathroom mirror. I zipped up my pants and snatched it, almost ripping it in half. "Fuck you and all the bullshit you put me through the last few years. A woman can only take but so much."

The words cut deep. I read the piece of torn off yellow paper once again just to make sure that I was reading it correctly. It wasn't like my wife to take such a tone with me. This was out of the blue and I was in total shock. I couldn't believe that she would pull some foul shit like this. "She must be out of her motherfucking mind." I threw the letter to the floor as if it contained some kind of deadly poison. I reached for my cell phone and dialed her number once again. If she knew what was best for her, she would answer the phone and not drag this out any longer. Thoughts of punishing her in the worst way occupied my mind and the longer she played this out, the worse things would be for her.

I paced impatiently across the floor while I waited for what felt like hours for her to answer the phone. After the third ring, her voicemail instructed me to leave a message. This indicated that she had either ignored my call or was out of the area. Both scenarios sent me into a rage. It wasn't often that she ignored my calls. The first time she had done something like this was the last time and I thought she understood that it could never happen again.

It was a night that I had been trying to reach her for over an hour. She had been out shopping with her cousin who had been visiting from out of town. I allowed the outing since they hadn't seen each other in almost ten years. When I heard her cousin's car pull up in the driveway, I hid behind the front door. I grabbed her as soon as she entered the house. She gave me some bogus excuse about how they were in a loud restaurant and she had missed my calls. To make matters worse, her battery died so she couldn't call me back. Needless to say, after all she endured that night, she knew that she would need to do everything within her power to touch base with me when she was out, no matter the circumstances.

I was seeing red as I drove through town. I was gripping the steering wheel so tight while imagining my hands around her neck. My mind was filled with the things I wanted to do to her but my main goal was to get to her as soon as possible. I rode through the neighborhoods of some of her family members. I also scoped out the parking lot where she worked. I even visited all of the hospitals, praying for her sake that she had been involved in some horrible accident and had been admitted.

With no luck, I turned left on Lucas Street where her best friend Paula lived. I knew that if anybody knew where she was, it would be her. Paula and my wife had been friends ever since high school and they were inseparable. Just shortly after we were married, I set some ground rules. I let her know that I didn't feel comfortable with her hanging out with all kinds of loose women and that she would have to choose one of the seven that had been in her circle. Paula was that one friend and so far, she gave me no reason to dismiss her as well. She immediately adapted to the lifestyle

I had carefully laid out for my wife, and best of all, she knew how to mind her own damn business.

I pulled into the driveway and jumped out of the car before I had completely stopped. The motion light came on and I saw someone peeping out the blinds at me as I made my way up to the porch. Before I made it to the last step, Paula was standing at the door with a forced smile on her face. "Hey Victor, what's up?" She looked nervous while tying her robe. "Where is she Paula?" Her live in boyfriend walked up behind her. "What's going on?"

I didn't know much about him but if he was a smart man, he'd mind his own business and go back to bed. "This doesn't have anything to do with you Tank," I stated as politely as possible. I truly had no beef with him and I was hoping that he would just disappear from the scene. I directed my attention back to a now scared looking Paula. She held her hand up at Tank to let him know that she was okay. He glared at me before turning away to leave the two of us alone. She must've known what was best for her because as soon as the door closed, she started singing like a scared ass canary.

SIX – ANGELICA

I couldn't wait for him to leave this morning so that I could make the phone call I had been so anxious to make all night. It was my girlfriend, Dina, who had recommended that I make the call in the first place. We were having lunch the other day when I mentioned my suspicions of my partner's infidelities. She had informed me of a top notch private investigator she had used that resulted in catching her husband cheating. I was skeptical at first but I was at the end of my rope.

There were only so many times a woman could accept the same tired ass excuses. I'd had enough of hearing that a business meeting ran into the night or that a weekend convention had required all of his attention. Just thinking about all the times I'd accept his reasons for not checking in with me or answering my phone calls made me feel pathetic. Only a fool would continue to believe all the things that he told me over the years. It was time that I put forth the effort to find out if he had been being dishonest. I had to know the truth. I needed to know if there was someone else occupying his time.

I decided that I would make the call just as soon as I was sure he had left the house. "You want some breakfast?" I called out from the doorway of our bedroom. He held up one finger while shaking his head no. I didn't appreciate getting the finger but I decided not to show my ass and let him have it right then and there. He made it known long ago that background noise was unacceptable whenever he was on a business call. He said that it was both tacky and disrespectful and that Bryson Jr and I were to abruptly stop any conversation until we were sure that he had ended his call.

I spent years running out of rooms when our son was too young to be told to be quiet. Because of this, I had allowed him to give me the finger but I was starting to question the real reason that we were told to keep quiet until he had finished his "business calls". This time I decided to stand in front of him and stare him down until he hung up. "Well thanks for calling. I'll talk to you later." I noticed that the voice on the other end sounded like it belonged to a woman. "That was my mother. She was calling to wish me a good day." He flashed me a half smile. "She told me to tell you hello." I found it a little strange that he was offering information to me that I hadn't asked for but I decided to leave it alone. My mother always told me and my sister that if a man offered too much information he was probably holding back twice as much. I decided to change the subject.

"Are we still on for tonight?" He looked as if he had seen a ghost. "Oh shit. That's tonight?" I couldn't believe the words that were coming out of his mouth. After all the planning and reminding I had done over the past few weeks, I found it hard to believe that he could possibly forget. "Angelica, I'll be there." He stood up, grabbed my wrists and pulled me closer to him. "I wouldn't miss your sister's engagement party for the world." He lifted my arms and placed them over his shoulders before placing a kiss on my forehead. It was statements like this one that made me think that I was being ridiculous for even thinking that he would cheat on me.

I had become consumed with the what ifs and now I was actually starting to feel guilty. I wondered if I had been overthinking and jumping to conclusions. There could be good explanations for the things that I was suspicious about. It was possible that he had actually been stuck at the office all those times that he said he was.

There was a part of me that wanted to just move on and let all of my suspicions go. The other part of me knew that I had to go through with this. I still needed to know for sure. I had to proceed with the private investigation. Besides, there was no way that my best friend would allow me to back out of it now. I took a deep breath. If anything was indeed going on, I was going to find out after the phone call that I was about to make.

He had finally left the house. I stared out of our second story bedroom window to make sure that he had successfully pulled out of the garage and onto the street. A tear fell from my eye as I watched him drive away. Reality started to set in and I wondered what the rest of my life would look like without him in it. I thought about my son and the close relationship that he had with his father. I couldn't imagine our lives without the man who we both loved so deeply.

My mind was all over the place and thoughts of what the future potentially held for my family were almost unbearable. I decided to make my move after I was absolutely certain that he had made it to the highway outside of our housing development. I knew it was a little early to be calling this woman's office but I was prepared to leave a message. I hadn't planned to leave my name simply because I still wasn't sure if I wanted to go through with it.

I had decided to make the call but there was still a doubt in the back of my mind that my man was even cheating on me. I mean, we had a child together and he had put me up in this mansion in one of the best neighborhoods in town. He even allowed me to quit my job and had paid big money for our child to attend one of the best private schools in our area. In addition to all that, when he wasn't working out of town, he was at home in bed with me. He really wasn't that bad and I felt ridiculous for even considering having him privately investigated. However, I had to go through with it.

I thought about ending the call at least three different times during the ten seconds the phone rang. "Hello. You've reached the voice mailbox of extension four-two-eight. No one is available to take your call. Please leave a message after the tone." I had to admit that I was actually relieved when I received the recording instead of an actual person. I had preferred to leave a message because I wasn't sure what I wanted to say or even if I wanted to let this woman into my life. "Hello," I paused, wondering if I should hang up or not. "I received your phone number from a friend who has used your services and I was hoping that you could help me as well. Please give me a call back at 410-555-3324." I hung up the phone abruptly after leaving the message and instantly wanted to take it all back.

SEVEN – FRANKIE

I had spent the past few years trying to live without her but no one had been able to fill the void that she left long ago. No matter how many times I tried to love someone, I ultimately decided that they couldn't measure up to Peyton. Before now, I hadn't tried to find her because I wanted to respect her decision to move on without me. However, I wasn't sure if I could continue accepting a life without her in it. My current relationship had been no match for what Peyton and I could be. I finally realized that I could never love anyone besides her. No one could ever be what Peyton had been to me.

I remained optimistic over the years, spending most of my days daydreaming about the day when I would see her again. No matter how close I would come to loving someone new, in the end, I still couldn't help but compare them to her. Her beauty, her laugh and her grace; all of it invaded my thoughts every single day. She was the love of my life and there would never be another person who could take her place.

Peyton had been on my mind heavy lately. She's been my first thought every morning and my last thought before

I close my eyes each night. Hell, she's even shown up in my dreams. Most nights I'd wake up in a cold sweat, horny as hell. I knew even in my dreams that she was the only person who would ever be able to satisfy my desires. I had become so desperate that I was willing to do anything to see her. I was also willing to knock down anyone who stood in my way. We were meant to be together and the thought of her being miles away from me playing house with some pretty boy and their children was almost too much to bear.

I knew that my sudden craving for Peyton wasn't just because I had been missing her. That was something that I had done for years. I had gotten used to wanting her and needing her but not being able to have her. The realization that no one would ever come close to being what Peyton had been to me was starting to get the best of me and it's been causing me think irrationally as of late. I was starting to feel like my need for her was becoming unhealthy and out of control.

My behavior had surprised me as I have been all but stalking the woman I loved so long ago. It's amazing what one could accomplish with a computer these days. I had managed to find Peyton on a website that was used to help long lost friends reconnect. Knowing Peyton like I had known her, she would answer my request to become one of her friends whether she knew for sure who I was or not.

I had spent most of the afternoon thinking of a name for my made-up profile. Finally, I decided to go with the name Mike Williams. It was a pretty common name that probably wouldn't raise up any red flags. We were friends with a lot of Williams' back in the day and she would probably feel that it was safe to assume that this was probably a cousin of a friend at worst. I waited all evening for her to accept my request to connect. While I cooked I had my laptop on the counter in front of me. I even took it to the mailbox and the bathroom. I did not want to miss the alert when and if it came through.

She responded at about a quarter to seven. I was officially in and I was ready to use my resources to the best of my ability. I started off by plundering through what the site referred to as her "background information". I viewed pictures of her children, Jessica and Bryson Jr. I also had the chance to finally see the man who had everything I always wanted. Bryson was the man that stood between me and the woman I was meant to be with.

In one picture he stood proudly with his arm around my first and only love. She smiled happily with her head thrown back and her leg kicked up in the air as if she was ending a superb dance performance. They both appeared to be happy but I knew better. I enlarged the picture as much as I possibly could. I stared into her eyes. I could see the hurt. The eyes that stared back at me were eyes full of dissatisfaction. I saw eyes that longed for true love, the kind of love that she and I had shared long ago. My eyes started to fill with water. I squeezed them tightly and allowed the tears to run down my face. I used my hand to wipe them away and focused on the man that stood beside her. He was in the way and I wanted nothing more than for him to be out of the picture, literally and figuratively.

I glanced up at the top of the screen and noticed that Peyton had an invitation to the public. For a moment I stood frozen staring at the screen. I couldn't believe my luck. She was celebrating her thirty-ninth birthday at the Hilton Palace tomorrow night. This was the perfect opportunity for me to pop up on her. I couldn't wait to see the look on her face when I walk through the door.

I spent the next few hours trying to decide what to wear for the occasion. It had been several years since I last saw her and I had to be looking irresistible. Finally, I had made my decision. It was one of my favorites, one that complimented my perfectly sculpted body. I could thank all of that extra time that I had been spending at the gym lately for that.

I pulled my crisp clean ensemble out of the plastic cover that it had been safely kept in for the past couple of weeks. I laid it out on the bed. "Peyton will have a hard time resisting me in this," I thought. I could see her now, trying her hardest to focus on her husband instead of the person she had always secretly preferred to be with. I couldn't wait to see how this would play out.

EIGHT – BRYSON

I was caught up. Here it was, eleven years later, and I had managed to successfully lead a double life without my wife or my mistress having a clue. Most men would have never allowed things to go this far with an outside woman. I know that it goes against what many would approve of but it happened so fast. It wasn't my intentions to create a whole life with my mistress, it just happened. One thing lead to another and she became pregnant with our son. That was the point where I made the decision to create a separate life with her.

I knew that offering her child support while I went back to sleep comfortably with my wife and two children was out of the question. In her mind, we were a couple. I had led her to believe that she was the only woman in my life. In the beginning, I really did consider leaving my family for her. As time went on, that all changed. I realized that I couldn't bear the thought of missing football games or dropping my little girl off at cheerleading camp.

I started to really value all that my wife and I had made for ourselves and leaving my family had no longer been an option for me. Besides, it started to seem like I had the perfect life at both homes, that is until now. Things were starting to become more complicated and I was starting to spend too much time trying to come up with solutions.

It wasn't fair to cancel on one of them tonight but there was no way around it. I knew that the events in which both my women requested my presence were equally important to them but I didn't know how I could possibly finagle my way out of this one. Bailing on either of them would bring huge consequences. I knew that my wife would probably forgive me if I was a no show at her party but I had to remember that if she was to get pissed off badly enough, she could find out whether the excuse I provided was the truth or not.

There was no doubt in my mind that there would be a requirement of some sort to show her that I was really where I said I would be while her party took place. My wife's workday never ended. She played the role of private investigator at home as well as at work. Even something as little as trying to find out who drank the last of the milk and left the carton in the refrigerator turned into a full blown interrogation. As for my mistress, cancelling on her has never really been an option. She was the one who was satisfying my needs sexually. I'd be a fool to jeopardize things with her and I wasn't willing to take that risk. It was nearing time for me to make my final decision and I was not looking forward to it.

The time was four-thirty which meant that my wife was preparing to have herself pampered as she did faithfully every week. She would have the works; hair, nails, full body massage, waxes, etc. This usually cost her about three-hundred dollars per week. The expenses used to be my problem but once I began my extramarital affairs, the excessive fees just became too much.

One day I approached her with some made up excuse about the firm and how it wasn't doing as well as it had been in previous years. I informed her that we would have to eliminate some of our unnecessary bills which pointed directly towards her extracurricular activities and pampering. While I knew she wasn't trying to give up her weekly trips to the spa, I knew that this would be the very thing she would volunteer to take on. If only she knew that her pampering money was going towards the upkeep of the home that I shared with another woman.

I looked at my phone and noticed that I had one missed call. I knew that it was one of my oblivious women calling to make sure that I was going to be where I was supposed to be, when I was supposed to be there. To my surprise it was my daughter, Jessica. I wasn't sure what she was calling for so I picked up to see what my baby girl wanted.

"Hello daddy," she said in a sweet voice. "Hey baby, what's going on?" I tried hard to get straight to the point so that I could get back to the important matter at hand. "Well, you know mom's party is tonight and I was just making sure that you were still coming?" I could hear my son in the background shouting out a message that could be for no one other than me. "Yeah dad, mom is so excited that if you don't come she'll probably shoot you in the ass with her three-fifty-seven." He didn't seem to have a care in the world that I might have a problem with his use of profanity. "Jess, tell your brother to watch his mouth. And, as for the party," I paused. "Wait a minute. Did your mother put you up to this?" I asked. "Dad, please don't cancel on her. You being there is all that she has been talking about for the past few days." I didn't have the balls to tell her that I wasn't going to make it. "I'll be there baby. Just save my seat in case I'm a couple minutes late," I said. "Thanks daddy!" I could tell by her voice that she was smiling from ear to ear.

I know how important the firm is to you but you are really going to make mom's night by being there. Remember, it's at the Hilton Palace at seven-thirty. We reserved the double dining room." With that said, we both hung up our phones. She hung up feeling overjoyed while I hung up feeling as overwhelmed and confused as ever.

I had no idea what I was going to do. I no longer had to worry about just my lover and wife's feelings. Now I had the feelings of my baby girl on the line as well. I had to be very careful about the decision I would ultimately make. I couldn't help but wonder if Peyton put Jessica up to this. Having her to call me to make sure that I was going to be there was definitely something that she would do. I can't believe I had just given my word that I would be in two places that were miles across town from one another. I picked up the phone because something had to be done. I dialed those seven numbers fearing the moment that I had to tell her I wasn't going to make it tonight. This was going to be a very special event for her and having me by her side was very important.

I felt guilty for doing what I was about to do but it had to be done. There was just no way that I was going to be able to keep everybody happy. Either I just didn't show up or I could let her down now. The latter would be better for the both of us.

NINE – PEYTON

I gathered my purse, tote bag and all the gifts and goodies
from the party that my colleagues had thrown for me. When
I looked down at my wastebasket I saw an empty soda can,
some old reports and the sticky note I had tossed in there
earlier. There was a part of me that wanted to reach inside
and retrieve the number before Diane made her daily
rounds. If I waited until Monday to decide to call this
potential client back, it would surely be too late. Diane
wasted no time on Fridays. She'd have the entire building
spotless by the time I would have made it to my car. The
woman didn't play any games when it came down to
cleaning. A few years back, we decided to connect with her
husband and throw her a surprise birthday party at their
home. The location was chosen because she cares for her
father who is unable to leave home due to a physical
disability. Each room in her house was immaculate. I could
say with assurance that you could eat off of her floor
without a second thought. She took care of the office the
same way.

With full hands, I reached down and picked the paper
out of the trash can. When I saw that it was not going to

happen without me dropping everything I had already carefully placed in my arms, I decided to give up. I put my mind at ease by telling myself that if this was really important, the anonymous woman would call back on Monday. Maybe she'd actually leave her name the second time around.

On my way out the door I was stopped by the switchboard operator. "Got big plans for tonight Detective Hainesworth?" She slightly raised one of her eyebrows and offered a half smile. "As a matter-of-fact I do. My daughter has made reservations at the Hilton Palace for me and some of my closest friends and family this evening. I'm on my way now to get all dolled up for the event." I said this as a hint that I didn't have all day to chat as the lonely geeky looking twenty-five-year old always assumed I did.

She had been known to hold anybody hostage who was brave enough to give her the time of day. We had all learned that something as simple as "how was your weekend" would cause her to strike up a conversation that could go on for thirty-minutes or more. She didn't care if you were on your way in or on your way out, she was going to tell you her whole life story and then some. I often wondered why her response was that she never had any plans. After all, she wasn't a bad looking girl.

She wore long skirts that went way past her knees and her hairstyle rarely changed from a pulled back ponytail but she had potential. I could tell that she had voluptuous curves underneath all of that Amish gear. The way her breasts stood at attention underneath her long, fitted turtlenecks made me wish that I was twenty-something again. "Well, I hope you have a good time," she said. Both happy and shocked to have been released from the conversation so fast, I quickly proceeded towards the door.

After finding my keys in the bottom of my purse, I pressed the remote control to automatic start my car. I walked for what felt like miles to the other side of the parking lot. I studied my key chain for the time to see just how late I was for my beauty session. It was now four-forty and I was going to have to put the pedal to the metal if I wanted to make it to the salon before five o'clock. As soon as I got in my car my cell phone rang and the caller ID read 'Hubby'.

I knew that this could mean one of two things; either Bryson was calling to cancel on me or he was calling to wish me a happy birthday along with an apology for not only being short with me this morning but also for not calling me back all day. "Hello," I answered. "Hey baby. Happy birthday to you. Happy birthday to you. Happy birthday to my baby. Happy birthday to you," he sang joyfully. "Thank you," I said nonchalantly. "What's the matter. You don't like my singing?" he joked.

"Bryce, you waited all day to call me and not to mention the fact that you were short with me this morning when I called you." I paused and waited to hear the lie that he had prepared. "Aw come on babe, please forgive me for that. I was actually in a conference when you called and I had about fifteen of my colleagues staring me in the face. I swear I didn't mean anything by it."

Funny how I knew that he would claim to have been in a conference. This is probably because that's what he'd always claim to be doing when he'd be short with me or ignore my call altogether. "Baby please don't be like that." After a few seconds of silence, I spoke. "Alright, alright. Just don't let it happen again," I said, trying to play tough, still not sure if I even believed what he was telling me. "Never ever again," he said. "So babe," he sighed. "I'm calling because I just found out that they need me to stay here one more night, something about one of the other guys having a family emergency. Now before you get all upset with me just let me tell you how I plan to make it up to you. I know I can't be there tonight but I have already made reservations for the two of us this weekend at that bed and breakfast you love so much. What do you think about that?" He paused as if to wait for a 'yes honey, that sounds fine with me', but my answer was far from the one he had anticipated.

I couldn't believe him. Even though it seemed to be happening more frequently, I still found him cancelling on me hard to believe. This time I really expected him to be decent enough to show up at my birthday party. "Bryson, you never cease to amaze me. I'd be lying if I said that I didn't know this was coming. You are just so fucking predictable. Your job has always come before your family, but this time, I have just had enough," I paused to wait for some kind of additional explanation, one that I was sure I still wouldn't believe. "Goodbye Bryson."

I hung up the phone and called to give Jessica the bad news. I couldn't believe that he still didn't have the decency to at least drop in after I had our daughter call to make sure that he was still coming tonight. I couldn't think of anything that could be more important than celebrating my birthday with me. What could be keeping him so busy that he couldn't at least stop by and show his face? I'm no stranger to him standing me up, even for important events, but birthdays and holidays were things that always took precedence over any and everything else

TEN – FRANKIE

I had been so anxious throughout the night. The only thing that helped to calm my nerves was digging out the old shoebox that was filled with the letters she had mailed me back in the day. When I left to pursue my career as an artist, she had stayed in touch with me for a while. Things were moving in the right direction at first. We had managed to keep each other entertained with letters and photos that we would send through the mail.

There were times when I'd please myself after smelling the sweet fragrance she'd spray on her letters. I never thought someone could keep my attention for this long without me being able to touch them. We had both entered a world that was new for us, but with a little creativity, we made it work. I found myself anxiously waiting for the mail each day because I couldn't wait to see what she would send along with her letters. I'd always make sure that no one was around whenever I would open my mail. She would make sure to write the words 'for your eyes only' on the back of each picture as if she thought I would allow my new friends to take a sneak peek.

Everything seemed to be going in the right direction

until the long distance relationship became too much for her. She started expecting me to call her every morning, during the day and every night before bed. I think she thought that somehow this would secure our relationship. She thought that if she had spoken with me often enough, this would ensure that I didn't have time for anyone else. At the time, I had started meeting people from all walks of life and they all seemed so much more interesting than what I was used to. Don't get me wrong, Peyton was able to keep my attention but not outside of phone calls, nudes and letters explaining what she was planning to do to me once we met again. I still had needs and with her being so far away, she couldn't satisfy me the way I needed her to. This was my first time away from home and I was more than eager to explore new things and sow my wild oats. I had more girlfriends than I could count, and not to mention, sex any time I wanted it. That was something that I wasn't used to with Peyton. She was a goody two shoes who wasn't too comfortable with stepping outside of the box. As a matter-of-fact, just being with me was a challenge for her. I can remember the first time we kissed. She immediately looked at me and threatened to kill me if I ever told anyone. She was afraid of her friends and family finding out that she had fallen for someone like me. It was a hard pill for me to swallow but I understood where she was coming from. We had come from two very different sides of town and her uppity suburban family would most likely have a very big problem with me and all that I represented. Even though I had been entertaining other people, my heart was with Peyton. She made it hard to feel this way at times with her accusations and silly arguments but I still saw her in my future.

The day that I received her final letter was the day I decided that leaving my past in the past was for the best. The words were so harsh that they seemed to jump off of the paper and stab me directly in the heart. For the rest of that summer I was haunted by the words written in purple ink on her pink stationary paper. I couldn't believe that she was actually willing to give up on everything we had fought so hard to have. This was all because I didn't call or write as much as I used to. The truth was that I had been busy. I may not have been occupied with the things that I was telling her I was doing but I had been engaging in extracurricular activities. There had been plenty of nights when she'd call and I wouldn't answer. The next day I would lie and say that I had been at an art gig that lasted until after midnight or that I had been studying with a group of students from my art class. She would act as though she believed me but I could always tell that she was highly annoyed. She just didn't want to fight with me while being so far away. She would often ask after our little disagreements if I'd gotten with another girl. I would always assure her that I hadn't but I think deep down inside she knew that I was miles away getting mine. I was away from home for the first time in my life and I didn't have to answer to anyone, not even her. Halfway through the letter I realized that she was saying much more than what was plainly stated. I read the heartbreaking sentence over and over again just to make sure that I was interpreting it correctly.

The words cut deep and no matter how hard I tried, I couldn't look away from the paper. After all we had been through, she was throwing in the towel. She was giving up on us even after all the plans we had made while lying on the hood of my car staring up at the sky in the weeks before I left. She was willing to abandon any thoughts of a future with me all because of a few missed calls. "Please don't try to contact me after you receive this letter. I'll be busy "drawing" with a guy from school."

I was ten miles away from The Hilton Palace and all I could think about was the look on Peyton's face the moment I made my way through the door. I had expected for her to be shocked but I knew she wouldn't show it. She was quite the actress back in the day and hiding her true feelings was one of her greatest talents. She could fool anyone, with the exception of me, of course. I knew her too well. No matter how hard she tried, she could never pull the wool over my eyes. I knew her deepest darkest secrets. I knew things that she would never share with anyone else. She couldn't hide from me even if she tried. I was inescapable and tonight I would remind her of that.

ELEVEN – ANGELICA

"I called that PI you told me about this morning," I told my best friend Dina. "Good. Was she there or did you have to leave a message?" she asked. "Well, I purposely called before business hours so that I didn't have to speak with her," I said. "And why would you do something like that?" she asked. "Because," I paused. "I wasn't sure if hiring her was something that I really wanted to do. So just in case I wanted to back out of it, I left a message," I finished. "Well, has she called you back yet?" she asked. "First of all, what's up with the million questions? And secondly, no, she hasn't returned my call yet. You think it has something to do with me not leaving my name?" I asked her. "Uh yeah. It has a lot to do with that," she paused and looked at me as if I was as dumb as a box of rocks. "Gel, this woman is high profile and she made it very clear to me the very first time that we met that she doesn't have time for games. Either you want to do this or you don't. She is so not the type of woman who is going to even consider calling you back if you leave her some vague half ass message. Remember, you need her, she doesn't need you." She picked up the phone and handed

45

it to me while she gave me a look that said 'if you don't call her, I will'.

"Hello. My name is Angelica Martin and my telephone number is 410-555-3324. I am interested in your services and I would greatly appreciate it if you would give me a call back at your earliest convenience. Thank you." I hung up the phone and turned to face my best friend. "Are you satisfied now?" I rolled my eyes. "I approve." Her smile told me that she was satisfied. "Now, we just wait for her to call you back. Since it's Friday and you're calling so damn late, I think it's safe to assume that she's not going to return your call any time this weekend. Now if you would've done what I told your scary ass to do in the first place, we wouldn't be going through this, now would we?" I rolled my eyes before responding. "Anyway. You know what? Speaking of names, you never gave me hers," I said. "Girl, do you know how long it's been since my divorce? I couldn't remember her name if my life depended on it. Besides, if it wasn't for me saving her number in my phone under "New life", I wouldn't have had that either," she said. "And what is New life, the name of her business?" I asked curiously. "Nope," she said smiling. "That is simply the result that I knew she would provide for me, a new life," she laughed. "You are stupid." I joined in on the laughter.

"Well, it's about time for me to start getting ready for tonight girl. You know Ayslan will kill me if I arrive less than ten minutes early," I said. "I know exactly what you mean. Your sister is a real control freak and I pray for you throughout this whole wedding thing." Dina had known my sister just as long as she'd known me. She had witnessed the way she controlled the lives of everyone around her. "Well keep me lifted because I am definitely going to need it." She gave me a goodbye hug and left me alone with thoughts that were unknown to her. I was careful not to show any signs of worry over whether or not Bryce was going to show for the party tonight.

I stood at the foot of my king size, cherry wood, designer sleigh bed, studying the two outfits that lay before me. Next to making the phone call to the private investigator, it was the hardest decision I had to make all day. I asked myself questions like, "Would it be the black dress that clung to me, showing off my best assets or would it be the two-piece creamed colored skirt suit that was more formal yet suitable for every occasion?" Since I loved them both, I decided to play a game of eeny, meeny, miny, moe. Knowing my history, it didn't matter which one I ended up choosing. I would probably still go with the opposite at the last minute.

I was standing in the mirror holding up the black dress in front of me when the phone rang. The caller ID read 'Bryce'. "Hello," I answered defensively, already assuming that he was calling to cancel on me. "Hey baby. I was just calling to let you know that I had to stop and pick up my suit from the cleaners but as soon as I'm finished here I'll be there to pick you up." I was so pleased with the words that had just flowed from his mouth to my ears. I felt like apologizing just for even considering privately investigating him. "Okay. I'll be ready," I said. "And Angelica, I love you." I felt ridiculous for thinking that he could possibly have someone on the side. "I love you too."

Nothing could have reassured me more. Here I was on the verge of hiring a private investigator to find out if my man was cheating on me when clearly he wasn't. I had to rethink things. I knew that Dina wouldn't understand and to be quite honest, I didn't care. All that mattered to me was keeping my family together. No matter what Dina had to say about it, I was willing to drop all of my suspicions about Bryson cheating. I wanted to just move on with my life and forget all about calling Miss PI.

TWELVE– VICTOR

After she was done confessing everything she knew about my wife's whereabouts, I peered over at her garage door. Through one of the small windows, I could see my wife's Jetta parked inside. The reality of it all made me want to pretend one of the windows was my wife's head and land my fist straight through it. I looked back at my wife's best friend and saw a look of empathy on her face. I wasn't sure if the look was because she felt sorry for me or if she felt sorry for the ass whooping she had just created for her friend.

She knew that I didn't play and that I had zero tolerance for bullshit. It still wasn't clear to me what had made her come clean about the whole situation but I didn't have time to wonder. There was only one thing on my mind and that was locating my wife and finding out what the hell was going on. I turned around and started towards my car without saying another word. I was officially on a mission and accomplishing it was the only thing in the world that mattered to me at that moment.

I was a madman on the road doing about eighty in a forty-five miles per hour zone. I didn't care about the boys in blue or even the possibility of running a few red lights and killing someone. All that mattered to me was her, the bitch who was about to endure the worst ass cutting she ever had. I was filled with rage but stable enough to realize that I was being irrational and in no state of mind to make decisions that would create the best outcome of the situation. Still, I didn't give a shit. She had to pay and anyone who got in my way would have to pay too.

Once I got back home, I packed a suitcase with a week's worth of clothes and other necessities that would get me through my stay, however long that may be. My anger was slowly decreasing but I still felt strong animosity towards my wife. I couldn't wait to get to my destination and look her in the face. I wanted to ask her what the hell she was thinking leaving me, right before I knocked the shit out of her. It disturbed me to know that she was capable of such scandalous actions. I never thought she would have the balls to leave me. There was never a day when I went into work and worried about her not being home when I got back. This made me fearful for the first time in our marriage. I wondered what was going through her mind and what her plans might be.

After my bag was packed I turned on the house alarm and started on my journey. Thanks to Paula, I knew exactly where I was going but what I would find when I got there was still a mystery. She could only provide me with my wife's whereabouts but she swore to me that she didn't know the reason for her trip. Although it was hard to believe, I bought it. I believed that she really had no idea why my wife had chosen to drive to a place that was miles away from our hometown.

I must say that I have had trust issues with every woman I have ever come into contact with, but for some reason, I believed Paula tonight. It was something about the look on her face that told me she was giving me all the information she had been privy to. It was a look of sadness. It was a look that showed me that she had missed her friend just as much as I had missed my wife.

After working all day and the trip I had just taken, all I wanted was to check into my hotel and take a hot shower. Lucky for me, Paula had provided me with a recommendation and finding a place to stay wouldn't be as hard as finding my wife. I had planned to get out later to try and track her down. She had left me without a proper notice and I couldn't wait to find her to get some answers. I wanted to know what she was thinking leaving me but also what she was doing here. I didn't have a clue as to why she had chosen this place to flee to after escaping me. As far as I was concerned, she didn't have any friends or family members in the area.

The first thing I wanted to do was ride around and look for the rental car that Paula had described to me. I knew that it was a burgundy Chevrolet Impala and narrowing it down would probably be a bigger challenge than expected but I was willing to do whatever it would take to find my wife. After the last hour or so, I felt like I was up for anything that came my way. I had enough adrenaline pumping through me to fuel a whole football team before the Super Bowl.

After riding around for what seemed like hours, my cell phone rang. I saw that it was my wife's number on my caller ID. I was more than anxious to see what the hell she had been up to. The fire I had been feeling earlier had turned into a huge flame by this time and she had called just in time for the flying sparks. "Hello," I said in an agitated voice. I wanted her to know immediately how I was feeling due to the fact that she had me out here on a wild ass goose chase looking for her. "I didn't call to talk, I just wanted to let you know that I will be by this weekend to get my things," she said calmly. "You'll be by to get your things? Cut this bullshit. Have you lost your fucking mind bitch? You listen to me," I said harshly.

I don't know when it was exactly that she hung up her phone but once I discovered that she wasn't responding to

anything that I was saying, I decided to look at the screen. Apparently, our call had ended at some point during the conversation. I was livid. This was a first for her and it only intensified my anger. I had to find her by any means necessary.

THIRTEEN – BRYSON

So, it was done. I had made the call to confirm that I would be by my lover's side at her sister's engagement party. She had no idea that she was up against me attending my wife's birthday celebration. I had no regrets as I drove up to the dry cleaner's front door on a mission to retrieve my three-piece Boltini suit. All I could think about was the look on my wife's face when I walked through the door to join her and the rest of our friends and family. I didn't want to think about the consequences I would face when the time came for me to deal with my lover. Truth was, she had become somewhat of a drama queen over the past couple of years. At this point, I was just trying to find the right time and the right lawyer to free me from it all. I had devoted the better part of my marriage to this woman, and in the beginning, it had all been fun and games. Now, things were different. All the recent drama with her made me want to give my all to my wife and grow old with her and our children. I wanted us to be a normal family, something we hadn't been in a long time. I wanted to get back to family game nights and beach vacations. Hell, I even missed the little things like Taco Tuesdays.

I wanted it all and I couldn't have that as long as my lover was in the picture. I could never be happy gallivanting around like I had been doing for more than a decade. I was getting older and the games were wearing me out. It was starting to require too much effort on my part and that had taken a lot of the fun out of it.

I wasn't sure if going about things the way I had planned was the best idea but I assumed it would be the best way of getting out of being with her tonight. By knowing her like I did, I was sure that leading her on until the last minute would be the drama-free way. None of that really mattered at the moment. My wife and children's happiness was all that I was concerned about. I had been neglecting them for far too long. It was time to give back to them some of the past eleven years that I had taken away to give to my lover and our son. It was time to put a stop to it all. I knew that what I had been planning wasn't fair to her but neither were the things that I had been secretly doing to my wife. I've learned that in this game, no one wins.

"Here you go Mr. Hainesworth. Total comes to seventeen dollars and ninety cents," said the clerk as she handed me the plastic covered suit that had been a present from my lover a few months back. "Thank you, Viola," I said while squinting my eyes to read her nametag. She was a stout woman who looked at me over her small framed glasses. She wore a messy bun that was held together by at least five pencils. "Keep the change." I drove off leaving the older woman who resembled my grandmother standing at the window grinning like she had just won the lottery. This had everything to do with receiving her thirty-two-dollar tip. When I drove off, I felt the vibration of my cell phone that was attached to my hip. I saw that it was Jessica and I knew exactly what this was about. This was proof that my wife had put my daughter up to calling me earlier to make sure that I would be at her party tonight. I was certain that she was now calling to tell me how she couldn't believe that I had let her and her mother down. I decided that it was best to let it go to voicemail. I was no good at disappointing my baby girl.

Even though I was actually going to show up tonight and make everything better, temporarily hurting her was too much for me to handle. It had always been that way. Ever since she was a baby, she had the ability to bring emotions out of me that not many people had the opportunity to see. She had me wrapped around her little finger and there was no denying that.

I spent the next few minutes trying to think of a place to go for the next hour or so before my wife's birthday gathering was set to begin. I couldn't go to the home that I shared with my lover due to my plan of standing her up at the last minute. I couldn't go to the home that I shared with my wife and children because I was supposed to be out of town at a conference.

I decided to call up my boy Kyle to ask him if I could come over and chill for a minute. Of course he was all for the visit. It had been a while since the two of us had the chance to catch up. Besides, he knew all about my lifestyle. If there was ever a time that I needed him to cover for me, he always had my back. He never felt comfortable knowing my secrets because he thought of it as betraying Peyton. He viewed her as a sister and knowing about the relationship with my lover was often times hard for him. He didn't approve but he was loyal to me anyway. He's definitely my brother from another mother.

FOURTEEN – PEYTON

Shortly after hanging up the phone with Jessica, I pulled into the parking lot of the spa. I was already ten minutes late for my appointment and I knew that my beautician, Kiki, was going to let me have it for being late once again. I swore to her the last time that I would be on time for my next appointment. I prayed that she would somehow sense that I wasn't in the mood for her shit today. Not only was it my birthday, I had also just been stood up by my husband. All I wanted to do was to sit in her chair with the latest edition of Beauty Excellence and disappear into my own little world.

I wasn't in the mood today. I didn't want to hear about anybody's business and who was messing with whose man. I didn't feel like hearing any of the shit that I normally had to listen to. I don't care what anyone says, hair salons were just a place for getting cute and talking ugly. I admit that there was a time when I would participate in the gossip but that was until I heard my own name.

A few years back, I was under the dryer minding my own damn business when I overheard someone say, "Shh, Peyton's sitting right there." I lifted the dryer and glanced around the room to find every woman either with her eyes glued to a magazine or talking about some off the wall stuff. I was too embarrassed to ask what was going on so I pulled down my dryer and went back to my reading. I called Kiki on her cell later to ask about the situation. All she could tell me was, "Girl, you know how people always gossiping about you and Bryson and how he can't possibly be that fine and be tied down with one woman. Bitches get real jealous when they see black folks doing well." Although it made me uneasy, I dismissed it as jealously and didn't think about it again.

"Well, well, damn it well. If it isn't Miss 'it's my birthday so I can be late if I want to' walking up in here like she's fifteen minutes early," Kiki stated as soon as I walked through the door of her salon. "Kiki, please, not today," I held my hand up and said in a stern voice. She looked at me with a serious look that told me she knew that I didn't want to be bothered today. "Let me get her to the sink, I'll be right back. Sit in my chair," she leaned down and whispered to me after sensing that something wasn't quite right with my behavior.

When she got back she started with the questions. "What's up with you sporting the long face on your birthday? Is everything alright?" I remained silent while pretending to be very interested in my magazine. "Does this have anything to do with you celebrating your last year of being thirty something?" she joked. After she saw that there was something way more serious going on with me, she became serious herself. "Well just know that I'm here for you if you want to talk about it. Alright?" She waited for a reply. I nodded to show her that I heard her but to also show her that she shouldn't expect too many words from my mouth this evening.

I usually felt beautiful and rejuvenated after being pampered from head to toe but today I felt the complete opposite. There was no magic massage or facial that could make my stress disappear. I could use a few shots of something strong. Maybe then I'd be able to make it through the next few hours. I wasn't sure that I could put on a happy face and smile in my guests faces like everything was okay with me. I wasn't sure at this point that I wanted to go. I'd rather ditch my party and hide in my bedroom for the rest of the weekend. I didn't want to be a part of anything that required my happiness or anyone trying to convince me to have a good time.

After considering going home and pretending to have come down with some horrible stomach bug, I made my final decision. Even though my husband was being an inconsiderate asshole, I still owed it to my children to be at my party tonight. I had to take into consideration all of the planning and money that had been spent towards making me happy.

I looked at the time and realized that my party was to begin in forty-five minutes. That meant I had exactly one hour to get home, change and get to the restaurant to make my grand entrance. It was always something my husband hated about me. I was all about making a grand entrance. I don't know who would want to arrive at their party at the exact same time their guests were expected to arrive. I had to have my time to shine and if that meant making people wait, then so be it. It didn't really matter what he thought about anything at this point. Obviously he'd found something that demanded his attention a lot more than I had. Dealing with what or who was keeping him away was too much to think about right now. I decided to concentrate on having a good time and deal with the drama later. Tonight was about me and if I was going to have a good time, I was going to have to put him in the back of my mind.

FIFTEEN – FRANKIE

I watched her from my car in the parking lot where her party would take place in less than twenty minutes. She was sitting alone on the passenger side of a white jeep with a pink license plate on the front that read Daddy's Girl. I wanted so badly to go over and reveal my presence to her but that wasn't part of the plan. The plan was to waltz into the room that she would be sharing with her closest friends and family and witness the look on her face when she locked eyes with me. I knew that this would be the shock of a lifetime and I yearned for the moment she would try to keep it together in front of her guests.

I still cared deeply for Peyton. I despised her lifestyle but that didn't minimize the love I had for her. I hated everything she represented as she played house everyday with him and their children. No matter how hard I tried, I couldn't understand how she could just go on with her life as if nothing ever happened between the two of us. I often wondered how she could forget her past so easily while I struggled for years to come to terms with the decision she selfishly made for the both of us.

While I watched her through the tinted windows of my

freshly detailed car, some fool sped through the parking lot. He was driving like a bat out of hell in a tiny ass sports car that he had to know was too small for his big ass. Him and his passenger jumped out and shared a few words before the unthinkable happened. My heart stopped as I watched my long ago lover jump out of the jeep and run up behind the two men. She embraced the one who had just occupied the passenger side of the sports car. Judging by the hug they shared, I felt it was safe to assume that this was Mr. Bryson Hainesworth in the flesh.

It was torture for me as she jumped in his arms. It took me back to an earlier time when she had spent the summer with her grandparents miles away. I learned then that a long distance relationship could never work for us. Just like in college, I took her absence as an opportunity to see other people. I tried to remain faithful in the beginning but I failed before she even had the chance to unpack her suitcase.

Summer Tidwell was her name and she had been eying me the entire school year. I knew that she was one of those girls who got around and that there would be no limitations when it came to the bedroom. After our first time being intimate, we spent all of our free time together. She was a freak and that was what I was lacking with Peyton. Summer wasn't afraid to let her hair down and that's what I liked about her the most.

Peyton would call a few times a day to harass me and give me the third degree about who I was seeing while she was away. She would even make up stories about how she had been receiving phone calls about me cheating on her. I didn't believe that for a second since Summer and I were very careful about when and where we did our dirt to ensure that we wouldn't get caught. She was also in a relationship and she wanted to keep our extracurricular activities on the low. I had no problem with that especially since I didn't have any real feelings for Summer. She was beautiful, sweet and she pleased me in ways I never imagined but Peyton had my heart and I realized then that she always would.

After their romantic embrace, Peyton signaled for the two men to go in the building without her. As they went inside, I considered marching up to her to ask what the hell she was doing leading this man on the way she had the past few years. I wanted to know how she could move on so easily and not so much as call me. I had so many questions for her but I had to once again gain my composure and convince myself that waiting was best. It wouldn't be long before I had the opportunity to look her in the eyes and demand answers to my questions.

She waited a few minutes after the men went inside to get out of the truck. She straightened her perfect fitting dress, fluffed her hair and prepared to make her entrance. From the other side of the small parking lot, I shook my head and laughed at the clueless birthday girl. She had no idea that she was about to come face-to-face with her past in a matter of minutes. In her mind, this would be one of the best nights of her life.

SIXTEEN – ANGELICA

I was starting to panic. It was now seven o'clock and there was no sign of Bryson. I had been trying to reach him on his cell since six-thirty but he wasn't answering. "If this man is planning on standing me up tonight!" I grunted through clenched teeth to no one at all. I tried to calm myself down by thinking about the phone call I had received from him earlier this evening. I was trying to convince myself that there was some truth to what he had said and that he would be home after he picked his suit up from the cleaners.

I needed to know where he was. I practically sprinted to my cell phone. I typed in 'cleaners' hoping that one of the names listed would look familiar to me. "Express Cleaners," I read aloud before clicking on the name. "Express Cleaners, this is Rosemary speaking," stated the woman on the other end. "Hello, my name is Angelica and I'm hoping that you can help me. My husband has asked me to pick up his suit today and I was just making sure that it's ready," I lied. "And what's your husband's name, dear?" The woman asked irritably as if I was interrupting her in some way. "His name is Bryson Hainesworth. His suit is a-," I was stopped in mid-sentence. "No need for the description hone. I know exactly who you're talking about. He made one of my coworkers a very happy lady about an hour ago," she informed. "Oh, he did," I stated, trying not to sound too curious. "Yep, sure did. His suit won't but seventeen dollars and something and your husband paid with a fifty-dollar bill. When she went to get his change, he told her to keep it. Sure wish I'd a waited on him," she said. "Yes, my husband is such a generous man," I told her while forcing a chuckle. "Well, I guess there's no need for me to come by then. Thanks for all your help." I hung up the phone and proceeded to get ready. Now that I knew Bryson had gone by the cleaners, I was sure that he was on his way home. He would probably be calling shortly with a bad case of road rage, cursing out cars that held him up in traffic.

Judging by the fact that I had watched back to back episodes of my favorite reality show "What Would You Do for Love," I knew it had to be at least eight o'clock. Bryson still hadn't shown up and that was starting to worry me rather than make me angry. I had called his phone several times but it was going straight to voicemail.

While I was contemplating going without him to my sister's engagement party, my cell phone rang. It scared the hell out of me when I saw that it was Kyle, Bryson's best friend. "Hello," I answered nervously. "Angel, it's me Bryson. Listen baby, it's Kyle. Someone broke into his house and I'm over here trying to help him with the police report and what not," he stated. "Is everybody alright?" I asked. "Yes, he's just a little shaken up. Luckily, Tammie and the kids were out of the house when it all took place. Baby, I am so sorry about missing your sister's party but I am going to make it up to you. How about we go to that bed and breakfast that you love so much?" He paused as if to wait for a response. "Bryson can stay over at T.J's for the weekend. They've been begging for him to come over lately." There was a moment of silence. "Baby please don't be mad at me," he begged. I almost hung up the phone like

I normally did without further investigating the situation but this time was different.

He had been acting very strange lately and I wanted to make sure that he was really where he was telling me he was. "Baby, it's just that when I talked to you earlier you were on your way to the cleaners and on your way home. I've been waiting for you ever since then. I couldn't wait to see you looking all handsome in that three-piece suit." I began talking in my sexy baby voice that he loved so much. "You think maybe you could pick it up tomorrow before we leave, that way I could have the pleasure of taking it off of you this weekend," I teased. "With you talking like that, I'll be at the drive through window as soon as they open in the morning." I couldn't believe my ears. He had just lied to me. I had proof that he had already been by the cleaners and here he was telling me that he hadn't made it due to his best friend getting robbed. This was all that I needed to know. There was indeed something going on and all I could think about was how Monday couldn't come fast enough. I was ready to begin the investigation and nothing was going to change my mind. "I love you Angelica," he stated. "I love you too."

SEVENTEEN – BRYSON

"Man, I don't appreciate you lying on my home like that. If something happens to my house because you bad mouthing it, that's your black ass." My best friend Kyle didn't play when it came to things like speaking negatively out loud. He believed that you could somehow speak things into existence. "Man, stop being so damn paranoid. Not a damn thing is going to happen to your house. What the hell else was I going to say to her? 'I'm sorry baby but I decided to go to my wife's birthday party, I'll see you tomorrow'." I paused and gave my best friend a look of seriousness.

"Man, I can't mess things up with her right now. I've been with this woman for over ten years and I've listened to the things her and her girlfriends talk about. Even the ones that are still married talk about what they would do if they ever got divorced. You wouldn't believe the first thing all of them agreed on." He stared at me with irritation as he waited for me to finish. "Man, child support. Hell the ringleader of the pack even passed out her case worker's business card." His eyes grew big as he continued to stare at me, this time in disbelief. "Yes, you heard me right, this woman walks around with her case worker's cards stashed in her purse."

This time I stared at him to see if he now understood the reason why I had no choice but to lie on what he sometimes jokingly refers to as his most prized possession.

"Alright man damn. I get it. Now can we get ready for this party? You making me just a little too uncomfortable staring in my eyes like that," he said jokingly. Just to irritate him while I was following him into his house, I smacked my best friend on the butt like we used to do in high school during football games. He quickly turned around and got into a position as if he was preparing to do a Taekwondo move. "Come on. I'll go Taebo on your ass. You don't want none of this." He started rocking which let me know that his left leg that he was using for balance was starting to give out. He's had problems with his knee ever since he was injured while playing in one of our high school football games. "Yeah, I bet if I kick you in the center of that knee, your ass will be laid out on the ground some damn where." We shared a laugh as we both went into the house to get ready.

We pulled up at the Hilton Palace and I could already see that the parking lot was filled with most of my wife's family and closest friends. My wife was well-known and well-liked by many people so I wasn't at all surprised that there was already a crowd. I didn't see her car which could only mean one thing; she was trying to make a grand entrance. No matter how many times I told her in the past that she should be on time, she was still all about a grand entrance. I never really fell for that grand entrance excuse though. That was just something she said to excuse the fact that she couldn't be on time for shit.

My wife made it her business to be late. I don't care if it was a ceremony at school for the kids or a funeral, you can always count on Peyton Hainesworth to be in the back of the audience.

I barely waited for Kyle to stop before I unbuckled my seatbelt and grabbed the door handle. It was one of the most uncomfortable rides and I was ready to jump out of his tiny ass sports car. I always wondered why big dudes always had to have such small ass cars. They sit up in there looking like a damn stuffed taco. It was fly as hell but I swear I had a monster cramp going from my ass to the back of my upper thigh because of the awkward position I had been forced to sit in. Also, the mixture of both of our colognes as well as the twenty car fresheners that he placed throughout was causing me to have a headache along with blurred vision. I tried to crack the window to increase my chances of making it to the party alive but Kyle didn't believe in riding without AC. "Man, what the hell you doing?" He would question me every time he even thought my fingers were moving towards the door panel to let the window down.

As soon as he parked, I practically crawled out of the crowded two-seater. I leaned over the car and sucked in a few gulps of fresh air. "Aye man, get your hands off the candy," he commanded. "Either this or I pass the hell out right here on this concrete. Man you almost killed me in there, locking the windows and shit. I should have farted I bet you would have had a change of damn heart then," I said. "Ah come on, it wasn't that damn bad," he said. "The shit you say," I said before straightening out my suit and preparing to give my wife the surprise of a lifetime.

EIGHTEEN – VICTOR

I tried calling her back as soon as I discovered that she was no longer on the other end. After several attempts to reach her, I realized that she wasn't going to answer but I proceeded to call anyway. I felt a tremendous amount of hurt, confusion and anger towards the woman who I never thought in a million years would have the balls to leave me. I never saw this type of betrayal coming from her. I really wanted to know what was going through her mind. At this point I figured she was either insane or she figured she was never going to see me again. Either way, she was either crazy or incredibly brave for going about things this way. I had finally come to the conclusion that I was only wasting time by trying to call her and that I needed to put more energy into finding her.

Once I got out of the shower and dressed for the evening, I took a moment to think about all that had transpired throughout the day. The events that led up to this evening sent me reminiscing about what got me here in the first place. It was the night of our honeymoon and I had considered myself to be the happiest man in Maui. I had the perfect career, perfect life and I had just married the perfect woman. I felt complete. I could hold onto that feeling forever and nothing could ever steal my joy.

As we sat on the beach that night I stared into her beautiful eyes. I looked up at the sky and thanked God for all that he had done for me. I wanted to hold onto this moment forever and I prayed for that. "You know, I thought I would keep this to myself but did you see the way that S.J. was looking at me this evening?" She smiled and seemed to blush. S.J. was our waiter; a young Hawaiian kid who also worked at the front desk of our hotel. I responded while trying hard to pretend like it didn't bother me. "Oh really?" I asked innocently. "Yes," she said giggling. "Every time you turned your back, I caught him staring at all of this goodness of yours." She sized herself up with the motioning of her hands. "He even winked at me today," she finished.

I tried hard to continue enjoying our night cap under the stars while the waves filled our ears. It was the perfect romantic setup but now all I could think about was some young prick trying to secretly holler at my wife right in front of me. I felt weak and disrespected. I had so much rage come over me that I wanted to march into the lobby and snatch his ass up by his burgundy tie and wrap it around his neck. I released her shoulders from the gentle turned firm grip of my arms. She turned around to inquire about the sudden change in my behavior. "What's wrong?" She looked confused. I ignored her question as I stood up. She stood up to join me and we were now face-to-face. I tried hard to harbor the rage that I had been working on controlling for so long but it was no use. I felt like I was about to blow a top that was packed with so much anger and there was nothing I could do to stop it.

"You prance around here in this little two-piece swim shit letting all of your stuff hang out and now you got the damn nerve to wonder why that little piss shit keeps giving you the eye." The look in her eyes was priceless. It was the first time that I saw fear in her eyes but that didn't stop me.

She was speechless as she put her left hand on her chest. "Do you wanna wear that shit or not?" I looked down at her ring. "What?" I could tell that she was on the verge of crying. It was like I was getting a high off of her fear and it felt damn good. "I said do you want to wear this shit." As I was speaking, I grabbed her hand and snatched the ring off of her finger. With my hand wrapped snuggly around her arm, I pulled it aggressively in order to get the ring from her finger. Just then I heard a male's voice yell out from the beachside bar. "Are you alright, Miss?" I later learned that the man was the bartender. She looked at me with her arm still trapped in my grip. I stared at her with a look on my face that told her that I was sorry and that I realized I had made a mistake. "Yes," she finally answered. "Baby, I am so sorry. I, I didn't mean it," I pleaded. She snatched away from me and walked towards her shoes that were a few feet away from us.

As she started back up towards the hotel, I ran up behind her. "Please wait," I cried. When she turned around, my face was covered with tears. "I don't know what came over me." Once I saw that I had her attention, I started laying it on thick. "I don't know what I would do if you were to ever leave me," I said. "Baby, I'm not going anywhere. That man means nothing to me." She tried hard to convince me that I had nothing to worry about. After that, our eyes met each other and I knew that I had her. She was never going anywhere and I was sure of that.

NINETEEN – PEYTON

I sat alone in Jessica's car outside of the place where my family and friends were waiting to help me celebrate my birthday. The time was 7:40 and judging by the parking lot, it was going to be a packed house. I wasn't sure how my daughter and son were able to reach most of the people that I watched walk by through the car window the last few minutes. I assumed Bryson Jr. had a lot to do with providing the contacts by going through my phone and social media accounts. The boy had a track record of figuring out my pass codes since he was five years old.

Just as I was preparing to make my grand entrance, I heard the sound of someone revving their engine. It was obviously a desperate attempt to demand the attention of everyone in the parking lot. I looked up and saw Bryson's best friend Kyle's candy red painted Porsche pull up. I decided to sit tight until he made his way inside so that he would be among the many who would greet me. To my surprise, Kyle wasn't alone when he walked by. Bryson was beside him. He looked like a million bucks as he strutted in a three-piece suit. I couldn't believe my eyes. He showed up after leading me to believe that he wouldn't and he was looking handsome as hell. I should have known that this was just another one of his tricks.

There had been several instances in the past when he led me to believe that he wouldn't show for an event only to make a surprise entrance. I tried my absolute best to sit tight and remain hidden but it was a failed attempt. I was so happy to see him that I jumped out of the car and into his arms. When I ran up behind him, he turned around and greeted me with open arms. "Baby I thought you weren't going to make it," I said as I embraced him. "Now you know I wouldn't miss celebrating my baby's birthday for anything in the world and damn do you look beautiful. Look at you." He spun me around to get a better look at my dress.

I was happier than I had been in a long time and I knew that this would be a night to remember. "Oh, hello Kyle. How's it going and how are Tammie and the kids?" I asked. "Everybody's fine. She sends her birthday wishes and she is sorry that she had to miss your party," he informed. I wasn't surprised that Tammie was a no-show. It was typical for her to disregard my invites. "Well, shall we," Bryson said while extending his arm. "Now, you know I love you and I am very happy that you made it, but having an escort is not my style. You two go ahead and I'll be in shortly," I said while creating a hand motion that would send the two of them on their way.

A few minutes later, I made my way into the restaurant. I stood in the doorway studying the crowd before approaching anyone. I saw people who I hadn't seen in years. I continued to scan the room when I got the shock of a lifetime. I couldn't believe it. Were my eyes playing tricks on me or was that really who I thought it was? Who knew to invite or even knew how to get into contact with such an old friend? I couldn't move. It was like my feet were stuck in mud or even cement for that matter. The old memories took over me and I felt like I was going to pass out.

Before that moment, it had been years since I allowed

myself to even think about that part of my past. I tried my best to pretend that I was happy to see everyone that was there but I was falling apart on the inside. I gave myself a quick pep talk and tried to mentally prepare myself for the evening ahead. I was determined not to allow my true feelings to show on my face and in my demeanor. As I made my way through the crowd I could see the face that I had loved so many years ago. I thought about turning around but it would look too obvious that I was trying to avoid someone. As I proceeded to greet my guests, I became nervous and a little anxious all at the same time. It had been a long time since I had seen the face of my long ago lover, and I have to say, I was very pleased. Life had certainly been good to that face; from the laugh lines to the beautiful pair of pearly whites that still shone like porcelain. I had no complaints.

"Hello Frankie," I said while extending my hand. "Now you know you'd better come over here and give me a hug." I looked around before leaning forward to embrace my guest. "So happy birthday. I have to say, the years have been good to you," Frankie said in a sexy voice while flashing a smile that immediately made my panties moist. "Thank you, thank you. I have to say the same about you," I said nervously. I felt guilty because after all the years I had been with Bryson, I hadn't allowed anyone else to invade my thoughts the way Frankie had the past few minutes.

After a brief moment of silence, I looked across the room and saw that Bryson was staring me in the face. I decided it was a good time to proceed with greeting my guests. "I must make my rounds," I informed Frankie with a disappointed look. "Well, I'm not leaving yet. Just don't forget about me," Frankie said. I walked away feeling a mixture of emotions. I wondered if Frankie knew that I had been married or even that I had two teenage children. I also wondered, which caught me off guard, if any of that would matter.

TWENTY – FRANKIE

Once I knew that she was safely inside, I prepared to make my own grand entrance. As soon as I got to the door, I could see her through the window. She looked as though she was comfortable and pleased with all of the guests that had shown up to support her on her special day. I walked in and disrupted her picture perfect world as she knew it. The serene expression that she wore just seconds earlier had turned into one that revealed pure shock and confusion. She looked as if she had seen a ghost.

Standing there with her eyebrows raised and her eyes the size of golf balls, she resembled a deer caught in the headlights. After the initial shock, she tried to greet me by shaking my hand. I wasn't going for that considering the history we shared. I responded by reaching out to hug her which she responded to with slight hesitation. After a few words, she informed me that she had to continue greeting her guests. I let her know that I wasn't leaving just yet before walking away to find a table. My goal was to sit directly across from her so I quickly scanned the room for a suitable seat. I noticed a table that was decorated with pretty pink and white bows and I knew it had to be reserved for her.

She had always been obsessed with all things pink.

Shortly after our initial greeting, she found her own seat, comfortably beside Mr. Lover Boy himself. "Look at him over there all hugged up with my woman," I thought to myself. It had been torture watching the two of them cuddled up so tightly. I just kept telling myself that pretty soon this fairy tale would all be over and that Peyton and I would live happily ever after. Once I had accomplished my goal, I would leave arm in arm with the woman who was meant for me.

I could tell all throughout dinner that she was trying hard to keep her eyes off of me.

Apparently, I still had the same effect on her as I had years prior. After all this time, she still wasn't able to resist me. Anyone looking from afar could see that she was bothered by something. Only the two of us knew what was causing her discomfort and that alone was turning me on. Every time I would catch her staring at me from across the room, I would think about the way she would lock her eyes on me during our most intimate moments. She was the only woman I had been with who liked to have sex with the lights on. She would make eye contact the entire time no matter the position she'd happen to be in. When she would use that tactic while going down on me, it would cause me to release immediately. There were times when I would have to look away to keep from letting go too early.

I watched him lean in and whisper something in her ear and I assumed that he was making sure that she was okay. She responded with a nod right before he stood up and said something that made my heart skip a beat. I was baffled when I heard the words escape his mouth. This couldn't be happening. This motherfucker had stolen my past and now he was trying to steal my future. I was seconds away from going into a full blown panic attack but I had to remind myself that this was all fake. Even though he was standing before me and an entire room full of people professing his love, I was unmoved. None of that meant a damn thing to me. I still had the truth to hold onto and that held more validity than anything he could ever say or do.

As they shared an intimate kiss, she glanced over in my direction. She was barely able to make eye contact. I gave her the most disgusted look, because without words, I wanted her to know that I wasn't buying the bullshit that she had been selling for years. I couldn't forget what we shared so many years ago. By the look on her face, I could tell that she couldn't either.

TWENTY – ONE – ANGELICA

As I sat outside of my future brother-in-law's home, I prepared myself for the many questions that I would be asked from family and friends who wondered where in the hell Bryson was. The questions normally annoyed me more than him actually not being there in the first place. Since I had been crying on the way over, I decided to check out the mirror to see how much damage had been done to my makeup.

After I closed the visor, I saw someone charging towards my car harder than Sophia did when she went to find Celie in The Color Purple. "I'm not in the mood to deal with this bridezilla tonight," I mumbled before getting out of the car. "Where have you been Gel?" she asked angrily. "Ayslan, not tonight okay. I have spent the last hour waiting for a man who assured me earlier this evening that he would be here with me tonight. Now I'm sorry that I'm late, but I really can't go there with you right now," I said with my hand in the air before starting to weep. "Come here girl. It's gonna be alright. Everything will be okay," she said with her hands gripping my shoulders before hugging me. My sister had been all too familiar with the drama I had been going through with Bryson lately. One thing I admired about her was her ability to offer her ears and close her mouth. She understood that I could bash the man I loved but she wasn't allowed to. "Just come inside, have a drink and you can stay over at my place tonight along with Bryson. Shit, you can share my misery as I sit through another episode of "Death at Scorpio's Inn." I smiled at her as if to say count me in. I always criticized her for watching the low budget series that she couldn't seem to live without. "Come on girl. I can't wait for you to meet some of my baby's groomsmen. Hell, if I wasn't marrying him, I would be all on top of them, literally." I playfully hit my baby sister before following her inside.

Damn, she was not kidding. The four men that stood before me made me want to disappear into one of the back rooms and let all of them have their way with me. They were all so beautiful but one of them damn near took my breath away. He had a unique look about him with his tall muscular frame and long dreadlocks. I was already imagining myself gently pulling them as we made love between my sheets. He wore all black, which definitely brought out the brown in his eyes.

As I shook his hand, our eyes met and never left each other. "Told you," Ayslan whispered in my ear as she introduced the two of us. "Angelica this is Jeremy. Jeremy this is my sister Angelica." As he shook my hand, he flipped it around so that I would see that he was trying to find evidence of a ring. "Good sign," he said as he kissed my hand. Right then and there I wanted to shout out the fact that I did indeed have a live in boyfriend for the past ten years but I thought about how stupid that would sound having been said aloud. I just smiled and allowed Mr. Jeremy's imagination to go wherever it wanted to go.

"Well, it's been a real pleasure getting to know you tonight," said Jeremy at the end of the evening. "Likewise," I said smiling. "So, is it okay if I call you sometime?" I stood there contemplating giving him my number. The way he looked standing there under the moon, along with the aroma of his cologne made me want to yell out those seven digits as loud as I could. "Look, I had a great time getting to know you as well and I don't remember the last time I laughed as much as I did tonight," I paused before sighing. "It is taking all I have in me right now not to lie to you, but I have to be honest." He gave me a puzzled look. "Jeremy, I have a live in boyfriend, and while our relationship is definitely on the rocks, I think it's only fair that I respect him by not taking this any further. I'm really sorry and I hope that you understand," I said.

I felt foolish being loyal to a man who obviously didn't care enough about me to even show up tonight. I was tired of being the only one in our relationship who respected the other's feelings. A part of me wanted to exchange numbers and meet up with Jeremy later just to make myself feel better. I was almost sure that Bryson was being unfaithful to me at this point. This time was different because I had caught him in the lie about picking up his suit from the cleaners. I knew in my heart of hearts that there was no break-in and that he had used that excuse to get out of coming to my sister's party but what I didn't know was what he had chosen to do instead of being with me.

"No, don't be sorry. I commend you for that and you've definitely earned my respect, but I just have one thing to say." It was my turn to return the puzzled look. "If at any time he stops treating you like the queen that you are, you look me up, alright." I smiled. If only he knew, Bryson had stopped doing that a long time ago. I shook his hand and nodded my head. "You take care," I said before walking towards my car.

TWENTY – TWO – BRYSON

After I caught my breath and got myself together, Kyle and I decided to make our way into the restaurant. Just as we started towards the door, I heard a set of high heels stabbing the pavement behind me. It was Peyton and judging by the way she jumped into my arms, she was very happy to see me. She was looking good, in fact, so good that I was already starting to feel bad about leaving her to go back to Angelica later tonight. After the three of us chatted for a minute, she commanded us to go into the party without her so that she could have her moment. After we walked into the party I noticed many different faces. Some of the faces I knew and some I had never seen before. I made my way over to my daughter and son first to compliment them on a job well done. Within five minutes, Peyton had made her grand entrance. Sounds of loud clapping filled the restaurant.

I watched my beautiful wife as she made her way through the large crowd. I have to admit that I was a little curious as to who all of the unfamiliar faces were. It didn't really bother me since I knew that my wife was in a business where she knew more people than I could keep up with. Hell, most of her colleagues were men and if I got mad every time I saw one of them in her presence, I would make myself miserable. I had to have trust when it came to her profession. Our marriage, aside from me living a double-life wouldn't be as happy as it's been for the past eighteen years if I questioned every Tom, Dick and Harry that walked up to us on the streets or called her business cell in the wee hours of the morning.

I watched from afar as I waited for her to finish with her greetings so that I could give her my surprise. As I waited patiently, I watched my wife's facial expression change from excitement to shock. I wasn't sure what it was that she had seen but after a brief moment, she seemed to be back to normal. I smiled at her to communicate that I would be glad to come over and rescue her from the greeting process but she just returned the smile and proceeded down the line.

She seemed disturbed all throughout dinner and I couldn't get more than three words out of her at a time. It was obvious that she had a lot on her mind. "So, is everything alright?" I asked her while secretly trying to make sure that the mood was right. I had waited long enough to give her my surprise and I didn't want to wait another second. I also didn't want to embarrass myself either. "Yes, everything's fine," she replied. "Well good because I'm about to propose a toast," I said before getting up from my seat. "Wait a minute. What kind of toast? Bryson," she said but I was already making my announcement. "Could I have everybody's attention please?" I asked while using my spoon to tap on my glass.

Once the room's noise level was to my satisfaction, I proceeded with my speech. "Now I won't make this long and drawn-out but I have something I would like to say to my wife." I tried to get straight to the point. I looked down at her beautiful chestnut colored eyes and allowed the words to flow from my heart. "Peyton, you are everything to me and spending these last eighteen years with you has been nothing short of amazing." I paused for a moment because for the first time since my father's funeral seven years ago, I felt like I was going to cry. "I want nothing more than to spend the rest of my life with you which is why I stand before you and our loved ones today." I got down on one knee just like I had done when I proposed to her the first time. Peyton Jalisa Hainesworth, will you marry me, again?" The crowd went wild.

No one, including my best friend Kyle, had known what I had planned for tonight and the expression on everyone's face was priceless. While my wife buried her face into the palms of her hands, I took the opportunity to glance over at Kyle. He gave me a look of disgust. It was a look that I had always hated. That combined with the slow shaking of his head always drove me crazy. I had become familiar with this look since he'd been responding to me with it a lot lately. He threw both of his hands up in the air just enough for me to see them as if to say 'what in the hell are you doing man?'

I didn't care what he thought about me or my lifestyle, which is why I didn't bother telling him about my plans beforehand. He wouldn't have understood the change of heart I had and the fact that I was truly considering leaving Angelica this time. I had confessed to him too many times after a few drinks or a long day that I wanted to leave her and the life that we had created behind. I knew that he would have to see it to believe it this time and I knew that I could show him better than I could tell him. I knew that I was truly ready to throw my double life away and concentrate on my family and that was all that mattered. All I could hope for right now was a yes from my wife and a promise from my best friend that he would stay out of my love triangle and allow me to fix it alone.

TWENTY – THREE – PEYTON

I could tell that Bryson felt my uneasiness all throughout dinner. Frankie was sitting at the table across from us staring me in the face. I tried my best to ignore that entire side of the room but to no avail. Each time I would look up from my plate, my eyes would somehow find Frankie's. It was like we had a magnetic connection and there was nothing that I could do about it. I went from being overly excited about this night to being anxious for it all to be over with. I had tried very hard the past few years to forget about Frankie and our life together but I always wondered what I would do if I ever found myself in the presence of the one that I loved so long ago. "So, is everything alright?" he asked. "Yes, everything's fine," I lied. I knew that Bryson wasn't too convinced that there was any truth in my last statement but that didn't stop him from doing the unthinkable.

Before I knew it, Bryson had gotten up out of his seat and made the most beautiful speech in front of all of our guests. I was absolutely touched by the wonderful, sincere things he incorporated into his speech but nothing could've prepare me for what he said next. "Peyton Jalisa Hainesworth, will you marry me, again?" I was speechless. I

93

definitely didn't see this coming. Before I knew it, I looked my husband in the eyes and said, "Yes, I will marry you, again." As we kissed, I glanced over at the very spot that I couldn't keep my eyes away from all evening. I made eye contact with a very disgusted looking Frankie, a look that made me even more uncomfortable. I felt transparent. Throughout my adult life, I tried hard to pretend that my life with Frankie never existed. Now, almost twenty years later, I was forced to face the reality of it all. My past was no longer hundreds of miles away. It was now sitting right across from me in a room that I shared with my husband, children and closest friends and family.

After I was sure that everyone had a piece of my birthday cake, I made a speech to thank everyone for coming to my party. "I would like to thank everyone for coming out tonight. I especially want to thank my wonderful daughter, Jessica, and my amazing son, Bryson for putting it all together. To all of you, I love you, take care, and once again, thank you." After I had completed my speech, I watched as my guests exited the dining room. I made my way over to Jessica. She was busy getting acquainted with my friend Gloria's daughter, I whispered in her ear and asked her if we could get going. "You okay mom?" she asked. "Yes baby it has just been a long day. After all of that partying I did, I just want to get to my bed," I lied while forcing a huge grin on my face. "Okay, well here are the keys, just let me go and tell Dad and Uncle Kyle goodbye." I nodded as I retrieved the keys from her hand.

After I had gotten halfway to the door, I realized that I had left my shawl sitting in my chair at the table. "Damn," I whispered to myself. As soon as I was about to walk back towards my table, I heard a familiar voice in my ear. "Is something wrong?" I turned around to find Frankie practically pressed up against me. We were now alone in the room that had just moments ago been occupied by most of my closest friends and family. I was praying that they had all at least made it to the parking lot. "Yes, as a matter-of-fact something is wrong," I said. "What are you doing here?" I whispered angrily. "Peyton, I didn't come here to screw up your little fairytale life, so just calm down. I just happened to be in the area on business and I didn't think it would be such a problem if I stopped by to wish an old friend happy birthday."

All of a sudden, I felt the gentle touch of Frankie's hand crawl up the lower part of my back. "You know, watching you tonight in that dress brought back memories of when the two of us use to-." The sound of Bryson's voice interrupted Frankie's. "You ready to go Peyton?" he asked. "Yes, I just had to come back to get my shawl." As soon as Bryson left the room, Frankie wasted no time slipping something into my bra. "Here's my card. If you ever get tired of playing house, call me." With that said I left the room, leaving Frankie standing there alone.

TWENTY – FOUR – ANGELICA

I decided to go home tonight. Although I was looking forward to watching my baby's favorite show with him and Ayslan, I just wanted to be alone. I just wasn't in the mood tonight. I also wanted to be at home when Bryson arrived. As I pulled up into the driveway, I saw that Bryson had already gotten home. "Wherever he had to go that was so special must have ended early," I said to myself. When I got ready to put my key in the door, I could see that he was sitting at the kitchen table. As soon as I opened the door, he looked up at me. I walked in the house and threw my keys on the table, pretending that I didn't see him sitting there. "Angelica, please sit down," he said. I knew what this was about. He was about to tell me that he couldn't take me to the bed and breakfast tomorrow after all. I was hoping that he also had an explanation as to why he was sitting here in the suit that he was supposed to wear to my sister's engagement party.

"Angelica, there is something I have to tell you and I hope that you can find it in your heart to forgive me someday." He rubbed his hands across his face which was something he always did when he was nervous. I wasn't sure what to think but I knew that this was about more than the bed and breakfast. "Angelica," he paused. "There is no easy way for me to say this." He rubbed his hands against his thighs before continuing. "I've just spent the past few hours at my wife's birthday party." My face went from an 'I don't care what you have to say' look to 'what the fuck'. It took me a few seconds to process exactly what he was saying to me. "Your who?" I asked. I let out a sarcastic chuckle. "What do you mean your wife? What are you saying Bryson? When? How?" I was at a loss for words. "I have been married for eighteen years, Angelica," he added. "Eighteen years? Are you fucking kidding me? But you live with me. Bryson, we have a son together. He's fucking named after you." I began to shake all over and my head started spinning. At that point, all I saw was red. "Leave," I said, my voice trembling. "But Angelica, we need to talk about Bryson," he begged. "Get the fuck out of my house you lying son of a bitch!" I screamed. Before I knew it, I had picked up one of my designer kitchen chairs and threw it at him.

A half an hour later I found myself still sitting in the same spot I had been in since Bryson left. Curled up in a ball on the kitchen floor, I thought about all of the lies I had been told over the past few years. I still couldn't believe the words that had come out of his mouth. I wished like hell that this was one of those times when he was lying or playing a trick on me like he used to do when we first got together. I had no signs of his double life. From the time I walked into his law firm over a decade ago, I thought he was the most honest, sincere man I had ever met. It wasn't until recently that I began wondering if he had found someone else but never in a million years would I have imagined anything like this.

I felt hurt, ashamed, betrayed and dirty all at the same time. I wanted to do something but I felt helpless. All I could do now was sit back while Bryson went on with his life with his wife and kids like nothing ever happened. I had to accept the fact that I had been played and no matter what I tried to do to punish him, I would only lose in this situation. I was fucked and although there was child support, he would still walk away a free man. I just wish there was something more I could do.

If I could just fuck him the same way that he had fucked me. If only he could feel a fraction of the pain that he had just caused me. If only he could endure the feeling of having his heart ripped out of his chest the way he had done mine. I felt sick to my stomach when I thought of all the times he had lied about his whereabouts when all the while he was cuddled up in his warm bed with his wife.

I got up from the floor and decided that a nice hot bath would probably do me some good considering the night I had. After I had turned on the water and poured my favorite bubble bath into the tub, I went into my bedroom to get out my pajamas and that was when it hit me. "Payback is a motherfucker," I said aloud wearing the biggest smile on my face.

I had completely forgotten about the message I had left with the private investigator on Friday and even though Bryson had broken things off with me, I still could use her services. I looked in my purse to make sure that I still had her number because if she didn't return my call first thing Monday morning, I would be calling her back.

After I made my way back to the bathroom, I looked in the mirror and smiled. "Bryson Hainesworth, you're going to wish you would have never met me when I'm finished with you."

TWENTY – FIVE – VICTOR

I thought that starting at the local hotels would be a wise decision. Before leaving, I had stopped at the front desk of my own hotel to check and see if she had checked in there. There was no record of her. I felt like a stalker trying to hunt my own wife down. I found it hard to believe that my search would be impossible. Trying to find her in a town with such a small population shouldn't be too much of a daunting task. After all, I knew what kind of car she was driving and I knew her taste in hotels. In this small town, I knew that all of the best hotels were more than likely in the same vicinity. This should make my job a little easier. It was starting to get late but I was determined to start my search tonight even if I had to end it earlier than I had anticipated. I had no time to waste and the sooner I got started, the better.

I pulled onto the road that was the address for many of the best hotels in the city. Almost immediately, I noticed that there was a burgundy Chevrolet Impala sitting at the red light across the street. It was dark and that made it difficult to determine if my wife was the driver. I knew that there were probably dozens of cars that fit this same description but I took a chance and went after it anyway. I made a U-turn and started back towards the direction that I had just left. Shortly after I started following behind the car, we approached another red light. This was my opportunity to try and see if the person behind the wheel was indeed my wife. I could see the figure of a woman through the back tinted glass but it was still hard to determine if she was my wife. I proceeded to follow her when the light turned green until she pulled into a housing development that looked like it belonged to that of the rich and famous.

I was beginning to feel hopeless at this point because she had no business being in this neighborhood this time of night, or at all for that matter. I was starting to think that I had been following some innocent woman home. "If this is her, I must be pretty damn lucky," I thought to myself as I turned in behind the car. I drove far enough away to try and remain anonymous. Once the woman parked and opened the car door there was no mistaking her identity. The woman that stepped out of the car was my wife.

"How was your first day back?" she asked when I walked through the door. "Nothing special." It had been a long day and I really didn't want to be bothered. "Okay, well for me it seems like I spent most of my day providing details to everyone about Maui. They wanted to know about the food, the people and even the water," she said happily. I was having a rough day and all I wanted to do was relax in front of the TV with a cold beer. This was our first real day as husband and wife. Every other day was spent on our honeymoon. She had yet to learn that when I got off work I didn't want to be bothered. I just wanted to come home to a quiet house. "So what did you tell them about the people?" I asked after taking a sip from the bottle I held in my hand. "Excuse me?" she asked puzzled. "Well, you said they wanted to know about the people. What did you have to say about dude? Did you tell them that this young Hawaiian boy was disrespecting you right in front of me?" I paused. "He wasn't disrespecting me." Before I knew it, I had smacked her across the face with my free hand. She sat terrified on the kitchen floor holding her left cheek with her mouth wide open in astonishment. "You listen to me. Don't you ever talk back to me for as long as you have breath in your lungs. Do you understand me?" She gave me a long, dark stare before nodding her head. I disappeared into the room to give her time to get herself together.

Later that night things seemed a little awkward between the two of us, as expected. This had been the first time I had put my hands on her and I didn't know what had been going through her mind. In an attempt to make things better, I went out to the store and brought her back a long stemmed rose along with her favorite chocolate candy bar. It was a peace offering to let her know that I was sorry and that it would never happen again. Once I walked into the bedroom, I noticed that she was sleeping and also fully dressed. I went over to her side of the bed and pulled off her shoes and then all of her clothing.

After sitting the flower and candy on her nightstand, I turned her over onto her back and climbed on top of her. I could see the bruise I had created on her cheek and I could tell that she had tried to cover it up with makeup. "Baby I'm sorry. I realize that I have real problems and I am so sorry that I ever laid a hand on you." I said all of this while kissing her from head to toe and judging by her body language, she was buying it. She started sliding around on the bed like a fish on land. She tried to keep herself calm but to no avail. I knew all of her spots and I was using that to my advantage tonight. The truth was, I was sorry and I had planned for this to be the last time something like this ever happened. I wanted a fresh start with my new wife and I would never lay a hand on her again.

TWENTY – SIX – BRYSON

After the night I had with my wife and our closest friends, I wanted nothing more than to change my plans from earlier and spend the night with her. I couldn't keep my eyes or my hands off of her. Tonight took me back to the days when we would cut our plans short just to get back home and make love. We didn't care if we were on a double date or if we had just sat down during the first 15 minutes of a two hour movie. If we got the urge, we would disappear with no regrets.

My initial plans were to take Angelica to the bed and breakfast like I told her I would but I couldn't drag her through this anymore. I had to come clean to her tonight and proceed with my life with Peyton starting first thing tomorrow.

The ride back to Kyle's place was a quiet one. I knew exactly what was on his mind but I wasn't sure why it had bothered him so much. I mean, after all he was my homeboy and he was supposed to support me in anything that I did. "Oh come on man. So you're not speaking to me now." Kyle kept his lips sealed and even turned up the music on me. I just stared out the window and prayed that he would one day understand why I was going about things this way. "I just wish you wouldn't have taken it so far. I mean, you've been with Angelica longer than you were with Peyton when you met her." I knew it wouldn't be long before he broke the silence. He was never good at giving me the silent treatment.

"Kyle, I understand what you're saying but just trust me this time. I wish I could turn back the hands of time too but it's a little too late for that and I want to give Peyton my all from now on. It's over between Angelica and I. I just want to be able to pay her in child support and move on with my life," I said. "And just when are you planning on telling Peyton about your other Bryson Jr?" he asked in disgust. I held my head low and rubbed my temples. "I wasn't planning on telling her at all," I said with shame. My answer must not have been to his liking because he turned his music back up and for the remainder of the drive, he had nothing else to say to me.

I just couldn't believe the way Kyle had been blowing this whole thing out of proportion. I mean, why did he care so damn much anyway? That whole 'bros before hoes' thing just went out the window.

I was so relieved to have been back in my own vehicle and on my way to the home that I had shared with Angelica. I wasn't too thrilled about telling her the secret that I had kept from her for so many years but it was now or never. I felt there was no need to drag this out any longer. I knew what I wanted my future to consist of and that didn't involve Angelica or the son we shared. It may seem a little harsh but with all the child support I would be forced to pay I knew that he would be well taken care of.

Once I pulled up into the driveway, I noticed that Angelica wasn't home yet. This probably meant that she was still at her sister's party. I decided to wait for her. I was hoping that she wouldn't be too long because I didn't want Peyton to start to wonder where I was. I told her that I was going to pick up my truck from Kyle's and make a quick stop by the office. I knew that pretty soon her PI instincts would start to kick in.

Shortly after I had made it in the house, I saw Angelica's headlights. I became nervous when I heard her put her key in the door. Once she was successfully inside, she made an attempt to walk right past me. I wasted no time asking her to have a seat so that I could talk to her. I didn't have time for her games tonight. I wanted to get straight to the point and be on my way. Once she obliged, I proceeded to tell her where I had been the past few hours and that is when all hell broke loose. I struggled to get a word in but I managed to fill her in on the life that I had before her and during our entire relationship. She became enraged.

For the next few minutes, she called me every name in the book. I wanted to just get up and leave but I wasn't finished with what I had to say. As I prepared to reveal to her that I also had two teenagers, she lost it. "Get the fuck out of my house you lying son of a bitch!" she screamed. I decided to do as I was told because I didn't need for things to get further out of hand.

The drive home was spent thinking about my new life and how ready I was to devote myself to my wife and children. All I could imagine was the night I was going to have with my wife. This would be the first time in years that I would make love to her and not imagine Angelica in the back of my mind. I was now a faithful one-woman-man and there was nothing Angelica or anyone could do to stand between me and my new life.

TWENTY – SEVEN – FRANKIE

I couldn't believe what I had just heard. This bastard had managed to steal Peyton from me once and now he's standing here making a commitment to do it again. I was disgusted by his words to say the least. I could hardly look at Peyton. She was wrong to have done it the first time around and here she was agreeing to marry prince charming all over again. I was overwhelmed with emotions and all I wanted to do was look into her eyes and demand the truth. I wanted her to tell me what I already knew; that she desired no one but me and that marrying Bryson in the first place was just to fill the void that I had left in her heart.

After the proposal, Peyton thanked everyone for coming and the party was over. I watched her as she searched the crowd nervously for me. I was over by the bar blending in well with a few of her colleagues who had no idea who I was. I listened as they all shared their thoughts on Bryson and Peyton's marriage and how happy they were that such a lovely couple would be renewing their vows. It took all I had not to throw up in the champagne glass that I had been gripping tightly in my hand.

I could see that Peyton's number one goal was to escape

the building without running into me. She glanced over her shoulders and peeped through the crowd of guests that were leaving. I could see the look of frustration on her face as she started back towards the dining area. She wore a look that represented an aggravated woman, one who couldn't escape her troubles fast enough. It appeared that she had forgotten something. I watched her as she made her way back to the dining room. I took this as my opportunity to approach her.

After I had successfully startled her, I shared a few words before slipping my business card into her double D size cleavage. I wanted to remind her of what she was missing, regardless of what she might have tried to convince herself over the years. She was a nervous wreck and that was the exact way I wanted her to be. Just as her eyes became weak and her body began to relax, there was an interruption. It was the home wrecker himself. He had come back to check on her. She had done a superb job creating a scene that would not be alarming to him. I was sure that he would walk away without giving my identity a second thought. Once again, another lie had set her free. My goal was to make sure that it didn't happen again.

After I left the party, I parked at a gas station next door and waited for her to pass by. I remembered the white Jeep that she had been sitting in earlier before the party and focused on every vehicle that drove by. My night was off to a great start and the real fun hadn't even started yet. I was desperate for this night to go the way I had planned. I could feel my body began to react to the dirty thoughts of my past and I rubbed myself for relief. Peyton always had that effect on me. While trying hard to concentrate on anything besides the body of my lover, I noticed the Jeep approaching the stop light in front of the gas station. I put my car in drive and slowly proceeded to follow them. I had to admit that I was a little jealous when I saw all that he had done for her. The house that I saw from down the street was more than I had ever imagined. "I knew that Peyton was doing well for herself, but damn," I said aloud.

Since I had already done my research, I knew that she would be alone tonight after her party. The social media site that I had recently joined in order to keep up with her had come in handy. I had learned that Jessica and Bryson Jr. were overly excited about a senior party that was happening tonight. This seemed all too perfect as it fit right in with my plan to pay her a visit.

I watched as the Jeep pulled off slowly and quickly gained speed once it was out of sight. She stood at the door and waved goodbye to them before quickly going into the house. After checking out my surroundings, I walked up to her front door. I had all intentions of knocking until the moment I tried the knob. The door had not been locked so I decided to enter on my own.

Once inside, I could hear movement coming from one of the bedrooms. She began to call out for Bryson and I followed her voice. My heart started to race as I got closer to her bedroom doorway. Once I had reached my destination, I found the most beautiful sight. She was standing there looking even more beautiful than I had remembered. Her naked body glistened as if she had just rubbed down in a bottle of baby oil. I was horny as hell and all I could think about was making love to her in the king size bed that was covered in silk sheets behind her.

TWENTY – EIGHT – PEYTON

"There's no place like home," I said as soon as I walked through the front door of my house. "Ma, you good?" Jessica yelled out from her car window before rushing off to the annual senior party. The event was held every year for the graduating class on the night of senior cut day. As usual, Bryson Jr was sitting right there on the passenger side. He was ready to ride just as he had been this morning. I was extremely blessed for them to have such a close relationship. They got along like two best friends. In fact, the only time they ever fought was when one of them didn't want to hang out with the other. After I assured them that I was fine, they pulled out of the driveway. I also assured them that they'd better not make me have to come looking for them.

As soon as I was sure that they were long gone, I rushed off to my bedroom. I was on a search for one of the sexy nighties that Bryson loved so much. I found one that I hadn't worn in months, maybe even years. While stripping off my clothes, Frankie's card fell from my bra and onto the floor. I picked it up and studied it. For a moment I thought about using it but decided against the idea. Instead, I stuffed the card deep down into my purse. What was I thinking?

I'm a married woman. I had no business thinking about Frankie the way I had been. I had to put Frankie in the back of my mind. Bryson would be back in just a few minutes and I wanted to be ready for him.

As soon as I got out of the shower I put on my robe. I made my way into my bedroom to get dressed in my lace nightie that left nothing to the imagination. I remember the day I bought this old thing many moons ago. I had been out shopping with Gloria and she had a buy one get one half off coupon for the Lingerie Barn, a tiny shop in our down town area. The owner had been a retired porn star who was now in her late seventies. She had us cracking up with her stories of turning tricks back in the day. "Don't let the wrinkles fool you," she told us. "I'm sure I could pull your beau if I really wanted to," she said while holding my left hand and studying my ring. Gloria and I shared a laugh before asking for directions to the dressing room. She had convinced me to try on a piece of lingerie that was so raunchy, I was embarrassed to try it on even behind closed doors. The little bit of cloth it did have was cream-colored and it came with a pair of knee highs that stopped at my thigh.

"You alive in there?" I heard the funny little perverted woman say. I couldn't believe that I was not only forced to endure the embarrassment of showing one of my best friends my naked body but I also had to face a former porn star with my breasts and ass exposed. I felt dirty walking out there flashing my ass which was only covered by something that resembled a spaghetti noodle. They tried to convince me that I was overreacting and that the only way to keep my man was to buy this piece of dental floss. That's the day I decided to start my collection of unused lingerie.

I heard Bryson enter the house. I snatched off my robe and tried to quickly slip into my sexy attire. "I'm in here," I yelled out to him. Since I had no time at this point to get dressed, I decided to stand naked in front of the doorway so that the first thing Bryson saw when he walked down the hall was me in my birthday suit. I knew this wouldn't be a problem for him since he always preferred me that way. He always said he didn't know why women spent money on night dresses as he called them. He figured why waste money on something that's only in the way and that's only going to come off anyway. I posed with my hands on my hips. My toned body glistened from the baby oil that I had just rubbed down in. I couldn't wait to give my husband the time of his life.

I focused on the person that stood before me. I was shocked and I couldn't speak or breathe for what felt like minutes. Frankie stared back at me. I struggled to grab my robe and cover up but my unauthorized guest had already walked over to me and wasted no time stroking my hair. "You look even more beautiful than you did at the party. Then again, I always preferred you in nothing at all," Frankie said. "You can't be here. You have to leave now," I said while trying to cover up what I could with my arms and hands. "Just relax. I saw the way that you kept staring at me tonight. It took everything in you to keep your eyes off of me. You should have seen yourself, sitting over there trying to pretend to be interested in the bullshit he was feeding you."

I felt exposed, as if my secret was out. Frankie knew as well as I did that there were still strong feelings for someone other than Bryson deep down in my heart. "Frankie, what we had was a long time ago. No matter what you may think, Bryson shouldn't be the person to blame for me leaving you. He never stole me from you like you've tried to convince yourself," I paused. "You gave me away," I finished. "When you left to pursue your career as an artist, I felt alone and betrayed. You seemed to just forget about all you left behind." I paused to keep from crying, I didn't want to show how vulnerable I was at that moment. "All I wanted was for someone to love me so that I could stop loving you. Bryson was that person," I looked down as if searching for encouragement from the floor. "And he still is." I looked back up, stared into Frankie's eyes and waited for a response. "Peyton, I know you don't mean any of that. You couldn't even look me in the eyes when that made up fairy tale shit just rolled off your tongue. That's why I'm here."

At that moment, I could feel Frankie's hands work their way up my exposed thighs. I felt like I was having an out of body experience as I reminisced on the times we used to share. I reflected on how good the love was that we used to make. My whole body trembled as Frankie's middle finger slipped inside of me. At that moment, I felt a familiar feeling take over my entire body and I knew that there was no turning back. I fell onto the bed and allowed myself to become caught up in Frankie's love magic. I knew all too well what this potion was capable of. As I lay back and allowed Frankie to please me, I grabbed both my breasts the way I used to many years ago. This always turned Frankie on even more. My body felt so relaxed. Even if I tried to get up from this position, I don't think I would've been successful. The two of us made love just like we had many years ago.

TWENTY – NINE – PEYTON

After we were both satisfied, I immediately felt a heavy since of guilt. My heart felt like it carried a ton of bricks. I couldn't believe that I had just cheated on my husband. I jumped out of the bed that I had just had sex with Frankie in and searched for my robe. "Shit Frankie, Bryson will be here any minute now. You really have to go," I demanded. Frankie stood in front of me half dressed. I could feel my body react just by admiring Frankie's best assets that were hanging before me. It was doing the total opposite of what my heart wanted it to do.

"Peyton, I'll go but you can't keep doing this to yourself or to him for that matter," Frankie said. "Frankie," I said annoyed. "Before tonight, you were just someone from my past, someone I had worked hard to forget about. I had no plans of seeing you again." My eyes filled with tears. "What we had was a long time ago. Now you have got to go." Frankie's hands began rubbing and caressing my naked body underneath my robe. "We could be so happy together if you just stop fighting so hard. Just remember how happy we used to be."

I found myself reminiscing about the good times we had. This time I leaned forward and kissed Frankie passionately.

When I pulled away, we both made eye contact. "Frankie, I can't deny the fact that we seemed like the perfect match. You were my everything but I have to also consider the life I created for myself after you left. Things are different now. I'm married with two children and I have no intentions of destroying my happy home," I paused and stared down at the floor. "I have to ask you to leave and I don't ever want to see you again." Frankie grabbed my chin and forced us to make eye contact before clapping slowly. "Bravo," Frankie said. "You couldn't even look at me when you made that little false ass speech. Now you might be able to convince everyone else in our past that you've had a change of heart but I can't be fooled. It's written all over your face among other places that you still care for me. We both know that you are not fully devoted to this new life you've been trying to live."

Frankie got fully dressed and stood in my doorway. "The truth shall set you free Peyton." With that said, Frankie left my home and I was left alone to carry the guilt of what was, what is and what should be.

It had now been an hour since Jessica dropped me off at home and about twenty minutes since Frankie had left. I had expected Bryson any minute now and I was starting to worry about where he was all this time. Suddenly, I heard Bryson's car door shut in the garage. With all that had taken place tonight I was looking forward to going to sleep more than making love at that point. I sat up in the bed and prepared for his entrance, once again.

"Where were you?" I asked as soon as he entered the bedroom. "Wow, you look absolutely beautiful," he said while crawling into bed. "I'm serious Bryson. You were supposed to be going to get your truck and make a quick stop by the office. Did you decide to work while you were at it?" I asked sarcastically. "Peyton, when I got to Kyle's house, he wanted me to help him install a new piece of software on his computer. As soon as I finished, I stopped by the office and got back here as soon as I could." He started kissing all over my neck. "Come on baby. This is supposed to be a celebration, let's not ruin it."

He ripped off his clothes exposing his milk chocolate muscular chest. He smelled strongly of my favorite cologne. He painted me with kisses while I massaged his manhood until it reached its maximum potential. "Damn, I've been waiting for this all day long," he said through moans. "Please don't make me wait any longer," he said while spreading my legs apart. He wasted no time slipping his hardened manhood inside of me. "I see I wasn't the only one anxious for this night," he said. "Your juices are already flowing," he finished. "See what happens when you make me wait all night," I lied. I knew full well that my increased wetness had been the result of my recent rendezvous with Frankie.

After a few minutes of stroking, I could feel his penis throbbing along my vaginal walls. It seemed like less than a minute before he collapsed on top of me. He was breathing like he had just ran a marathon. "Baby," he managed to say. "Please forgive me for not waiting for you this time. I promise I'll make it up to you. Just give me a few minutes," he joked. If only he knew that my needs had already been met.

THIRTY – FRANKIE

Just like I had planned, we made love. Shortly after I whispered a few sweet nothings in her ear, she was face down and ass up in the bed that she shared with her husband. Of course she tried to put up a fight, trying to convince me that she was in love with Bryson and that I was only someone from her past. I wasn't convinced and I told her that. The way she really felt about the two of us being alone for the first time in decades was written all over her body. She couldn't hide her true feelings. It was all in the way her nipples began to swell right before my eyes. Another dead giveaway was the way her breathing became slow and heavy. She wanted me just as much as I wanted her and there was nothing that she could say to convince me otherwise. She eventually dropped the whole good girl act and gave in.

She collapsed onto the bed as if she had lost the ability to stand on her own. This allowed me to kiss her from her breasts down to her toes. I remember how much she loved foreplay back in the day. She started squirming as if the teasing had become too much for her. I had her right where I wanted her, at a point of no return. I used to love when she would get so lost in the moment that she'd become weak, unable to do anything other than go with the flow. She'd put all of her trust in me and the thought alone only increased my desire for her.

I made my way back up to her middle and decided to kiss around her sweet spot. This drove her crazy and she began to jerk. Her moans started to fill the room. This confirmed that she had missed me just as much as I had missed her. I reached between her legs to determine if my hard work had paid off in all areas. She was just as wet as I had remembered.

After a few moments of intense rubbing, I slipped one finger inside of her. She opened her legs before doing a swirling thing with her hips. She reached down and grabbed me by the wrist before trying to stuff me inside of her. I slipped in two more fingers and allowed her to control the speed. "Oh Frankie," she moaned. Just as she was starting to shake all over, I removed my fingers from her center and replaced them with my tongue. I reached up and cupped one of her firm breasts with my hand while continuing to get the job done down south. She seemed to be enjoying what she had been missing out on for so long. I didn't want to interrupt but I also wanted in on all the fun.

I lifted her up while I laid back on the bed. I then turned her around so that I was face-to-face with her middle and she was face-to-face with mine. With her now returning the favor, my own moans filled the room. I had been waiting for this moment for years and I couldn't even begin to describe the pleasure that I felt at that moment. I was in ecstasy and nothing else mattered. With one motion, I helped her turn around so that we could prepare for the grand finale. She positioned herself properly and the rest is history. As we pumped harder, we screamed each other's names. I wanted to hold onto this feeling forever, but all too soon, it was over.

Immediately after we made love she started being all

anti-Frankie again. I hadn't planned for this reaction. As fairy tale as it may seem, I thought we'd make love and ride off into the sunset together. I had convinced myself that she'd forget all about Bryson and their phony marriage. I wasn't prepared for this outcome so there was no plan B.

After I left her, I spent the entire ride home thinking about her words. I actually started to wonder if there was any truth in them. I wondered if I should just leave Peyton in my past and move on with my future. However, to leave would be to allow her to live with a lie for the rest of her life and I wasn't willing to do that. We belonged together and no matter what she may have thought, that was the truth. I wasn't willing to leave here as heartbroken as I was when I came. Either I was leaving with her or I was staying here with her. One way or the other, I would have her.

THIRTY – ONE – ANGELICA

"What could be so important this early in the morning?" I asked myself while squinting at the numbers on the clock across the room. "I know somebody better have a good reason," I said once I had a confirmation that it was eight-twenty-four in the morning. "Yes?" I said in a frustrated tone. "Hello. May I speak with Ms. Angelica Martin, please?" At this point, I started coming to my senses and I knew exactly who this was. I cleared my throat. "Good morning. This is she. How are you?" I asked in a softer tone. "I'm well. I see that you left me a message. Were you calling to inquire about my services?" she asked, getting straight to the point. "Yes, I'm hoping to find out if my-." I was stopped in midsentence. "Please Ms. Martin, I don't discuss anything over the phone. Can you meet me, say," she paused as if to check her calendar for a good day and time. "You know what?" she asked rhetorically. "I'm actually free today around twelve-thirty. How about we meet at Jackson's Bistro?" she finished. "That will work for me," I agreed. "And Ms. Martin, please bring a photo of the accused. I prefer a self-portrait but if a close snapshot is all you have, that will be fine also," she stated before ending the call.

I was so proud of myself for what I was about to do. I had just arranged a meeting with an actual private investigator. I no longer needed her help to find out if Bryson was cheating on me. I now needed her help identifying the woman who he had been married to throughout our entire relationship. I was well on my way to informing his wife of the cheating monster in her bed. As much as I wasn't looking forward to the possible disintegration of a family, I needed this woman to know what her husband had been up to for the past several years. It wasn't fair to me but it also wasn't fair to her. Neither one of us were winners in this situation.

All of a sudden I realized that there was only one problem. Bryson always ran off whenever he was about to have his picture taken. He had me convinced with his exaggerations of being non-photogenic. He always told me stories about when he was a kid and his classmates would tease him about his school pictures. He would all but freak out in the past when I would ask him to take family portraits. He even ran away from the camera when I would ask to take a simple snap shot while we were on our family vacations. When I look back now, I can't believe I had been so naïve. There were so many lines I never read between and so many red flags that were slapping me in the face. Yet, I ignored them all. Now, I'm alone and heartbroken with a ten-year-old to raise by myself.

I laid in bed trying hard to go back to sleep but I couldn't. I was overwhelmed by the anticipation of meeting up with the PI. I couldn't wait to be face-to-face with the woman who had been my competition all these years and didn't even know it. I was so anxious to tell this stranger about all the times her husband claimed to be working late. I began rehearsing what I would say to her whenever we did finally meet. I imagined the look on her face once I revealed that we both have a ten-year-old son that is named after her husband. I wasn't looking to gain Bryson back by doing any of this but I did want him to feel what I was feeling. If I couldn't be happy, neither should he, or his wife for that matter. None of it was fair. My son would now grow up without his father and I had to accept that marriage was not in the cards for us. Hell, he was married. I still couldn't believe it. "Bryson is married." I tried to say it aloud to make it make sense. It baffled me that he had a whole family while living what seemed like a normal life with me. I may need therapy after it was all said and done because I never saw this coming and there was no way that I could have possibly prepared myself for it. Maybe my friend Dina would know the name of a good therapist as well.

THIRTY – TWO – BRYSON

When I arrived at work, I took a moment before getting out of my truck to thank God for giving me another chance with my family. I'll be the first to say that I don't deserve another chance. I broke all the rules. I stopped taking care of home to be with another woman and I got her pregnant. My behavior went against everything that I believed in but it all happened so fast.

One day she was my new assistant and shortly after, we were playing house with a son that I allowed to be named after me. I don't know what I thought would come of this or how long I actually expected this to go on but I always knew that it was wrong. No matter how you look at it, it shouldn't have happened. I tried convincing myself many days that I was entitled to a little something on the side because I wasn't getting all that I thought I deserved at home. My wife had stretched herself too thin and had taken on too many responsibilities outside of our home. I suffered in the process.

After late nights at the office, she'd come home with little to nothing left for me. Rejection had become something that I was used to until the moment I stopped asking for it. I started waiting for her to offer it up but she'd go several days before she'd even mention sex. When she would bring it up, she'd always make me feel like the worst person in the world for wanting it. I was tired of my needs not being considered. Once I crossed the line for the very first time, there was no stopping me. I had gotten used to someone wanting me and showing me appreciation. She didn't complain about anything that I asked her to do. Our intimate moments were about making sure that I had been pleased in the best way possible when we were done. I must say that the past few years had changed my life. In some ways, I think that Angelica saved my marriage. She kept me young and as much as I hate to admit it, she kept me happy. Breaking things off with her wasn't something that I looked forward to but it didn't go as bad as I had anticipated. She was upset but the good thing was that she had no prior knowledge of my other life. Thankfully, she couldn't drive by my house or call Peyton up to inform her of my deceit. I had already decided that I would give her some time to cool off before reaching out to set up arrangements for child support. I'm hoping that she will agree to keep the courts out of the process.

It was a pure blessing that I was able to pick up things where I left off with Peyton without her even knowing anything was going on in the first place. I also prayed to eventually continue having a relationship with Bryson Jr. I hoped that his mother wouldn't try to make my life a living hell because of what I did to her. I never understood why women would use their children to get back at men for doing them wrong. Ultimately, the children are the ones that suffer. I wasn't sure what Angelica would do to try and get back at me but I was sure that it would not be her idea. It would be something that her scandalous ass friends would put her up to. I could picture them now gathering around her in a circle trying to convince her to get me for all I'm worth.

After I grabbed a cup of coffee and checked my messages, I decided to check in with Peyton. "Well hello there," I said after she greeted me. "How's your day going so far?" I asked. "I can't complain. I've already managed to figure out a way to work through my lunch today," she said. "Well, that doesn't surprise me one bit," I said. "Hey, I have to support my spa habits somehow. You're the one who cut me off, which is the reason why I decided to do the PI thing part-time in the first place. Remember?" she asked sarcastically. "About that, the firm has been doing a lot better lately and I should be able to start giving you your allowances again. Effective immediately," I lied.

The truth was, now that I didn't have to support two households, I could afford to take care of my wife in all areas the way I used to. Speaking of which, I had come up with a financial plan that would allow me to pay Angelica almost half of what I used to. I knew she wouldn't like the idea of having to move out of house and get a job but she had no other choice. I just hoped she didn't jump stupid after receiving the news.

"Now that's what I'm talking about," she said. I could hear her clapping in the background. "Bryson, I'm not sure what has brought about such a change in you but I like it. I might just make my current case my last PI gig," she said. "Well I guess I better get going. Alice is taking orders for lunch and I guess now that you've turned me down, I better go and put mine in," I said. "Oh babe, I didn't know. How about we set a lunch date for tomorrow," she offered. "Alright, I'll take it," I agreed before ending the call.

THIRTY – THREE –VICTOR

I watched as she got out of the vehicle and walked up the driveway. She seemed to be familiar with her surroundings because she didn't look around to see who was watching. She entered the beautiful mansion without knocking as if she knew where she was going. She didn't even look back. I sat in my car confused, watching helplessly. She was all dressed up in the two-piece cream colored suit that I always loved seeing her in. Once she was inside, she closed the door behind her. I had a hard time believing that she had already managed to find a home this nice since she had just arrived a day prior. Either she had been planning to leave me for some time now or she had a bomb ass realtor.

At this point, I had forgotten about all the reminiscing I had done earlier. Memories of the good times no longer clouded my vision and I was able to focus on the extreme rage that I had towards my wife. Seeing her brought back all of the anger I had felt for her before. I wanted to jump out of the car and do what I had come here to do. I wanted to drag her back home screaming and crying while demanding answers from her. After all she put me through I wasn't sure why I was still sitting here instead of in her face confronting her. I assumed that this was where she was going to be staying for the night so I made myself comfortable.

My eyes were struggling to stay open. It had been a long day and the emotional stress was taking a toll on me. It wasn't long before I saw the red glow from her break lights through my eyelids. She had been inside for a little over thirty minutes and now she was leaving. I wondered where she was going this time of night and also what she was doing at this house in the first place. I waited for her to turn the block before I started my engine and proceeded to follow her.

I stayed as close as I could to her as she made one turn after another. The area was becoming more and more familiar to me. Once she made a final left turn, it had been confirmed. My wife and I were staying at the same hotel. I chuckled as I pulled into the hotel parking lot behind her.

I had planned to go up to my room after I was sure she was safely inside and out of sight. I had come too close to finding out what her business was in this town and I didn't want to blow it. When she got out of her car I slid down in my seat to make sure that she didn't notice that it was me sitting inside. Even though I had discreetly parked across the parking lot, I thought I couldn't be too careful. After she gathered her things from inside the car, I started preparing for my own exit. When I arrived inside the hotel a couple of minutes after she had, I cautiously took the elevator up to my room. My next challenge would be finding out exactly where she was staying. I had to be sure not to run into her during our stay here until I had gathered all of the information I had come for. I had already decided that before I confronted her I had to be sure of her reasons for being here. That way she couldn't lie to me about it later.

When the front desk clerk answered the phone, I could tell that she was probably wondering what the hell someone could possibly want at this hour. She answered with irritation, as if she wanted to make me fully aware of how my call was interrupting her. She was probably doing the same thing she was doing when I entered the hotel earlier; playing games on her phone. I proceeded with my plan of asking her for my wife's information. I had already come up with a lie in the event that she refused to give it to me. I had no need for a plan B because the impatient young woman was willing to do anything to end the call and go back to playing her games.

Within seconds, I was provided with my wife's hotel room number and the day she was planning to check out. This allowed me the opportunity to keep an eye out on her without worrying about bumping into her. With such progress, I was ready to lay down and get some sleep. I had a busy day ahead of me and I needed to approach it with a clear mind. I had no idea when she was planning to wake up in the morning or where she was going so it was imperative that I was ready to go bright and early.

THIRTY – FOUR – PEYTON

When her friend told her that she used my services she should have also told her that I didn't tolerate lateness," I thought while sitting at a corner table at Jackson's Bistro. It was now twelve-forty and I had begun contemplating walking out. I decided to give Ms. Martin until twelve-forty-five before I called it quits and she didn't have to worry about using my services in the future. I used the next few minutes to evaluate all that had been going through my mind the past few days. The thought of Frankie and all that we had done made me squirm in my seat. I still hadn't forgiven myself for the things we did that night. The realization hit me hard the next day and I found myself confused, like I was caught in the middle of a love triangle that my husband didn't know he was a part of. I spent that whole night staring at the ceiling thinking while I listened to Bryson snore louder than I believe he had in years.

At one point I looked at him and my eyes filled with tears. I had betrayed him in the worst way possible. I had cheated on him in our bed. How could I let this happen? As I stared at him, I thought about how good he was to me lately and I wondered what had brought about the sudden change. He had gone from working late most nights and cutting our phone conversations short to being more present and making attempts to spending more time with me and the kids. Whatever brought about the sudden change, I was here for it, but the thought alone made the guilt even harder to bear.

I looked at my phone and realized that I had waited long enough. I gathered my things and started towards the door. I was stopped by a waitress on my way out. "Ma'am, your guest has arrived and she's waiting for you at the table of your choice." I turned to look at the table I had just abandoned to see my client sitting there. She must have entered through the opposite door just as I had gotten up to leave. "Thank you," I said to the waitress before turning away.

Once I made it to the table, I extended my hand towards my future client. "Hello Ms. Martin. I see you finally decided to join me and you're only twenty minutes late," I said sarcastically. "Please forgive me. Believe it or not, I have spent the last few hours trying to develop old film, in hopes of finding a picture of my boyfriend, well ex-boyfriend," she informed me while lifting up the manila envelope that sat on the table before her. "Let's just get started," I said irritably. "Please tell me exactly why you've decided to contact me while you fill out this application," I said while pulling an application from my briefcase. "Okay, well to start, I have been involved with this man for the past ten years. We met when I was hired on as his secretary. Immediately we realized that there was chemistry between the two of us. I became pregnant with our ten-year-old son. At that time, we decided to move in together. Things seemed to be wonderful in the beginning and even towards the end. It wasn't until the past year or so that I noticed a change in him. He started acting differently towards me. He seemed to run out of things to say and he started having way too many things going on at the office. He even seemed to lose interest in sex. To make a long story short, a few days ago, he said the unthinkable to me," she paused. "He informed me that he was leaving me for his wife." She tried hard to pull herself together but was having a hard time doing so. He left me to raise our ten-year-old son by myself along with a mortgage that he had promised to always take care of." She paused and looked as if she was trying hard to hold back tears. "I originally called you because I wanted to know if he was cheating on me, but after Friday, I no longer need your services for that reason.

Her tears began to race down her cheeks as the pain seemed to become harder to deal with. "He confessed to me that he had been married the entire time we were together." All of a sudden her mood changed. She went from hurt to angry while wiping her tears away as if they were pure venom. "But now, I'm in need of your services so that I can inform his wife of his infidelities. I don't think any woman deserves to be treated this way. She deserves to know the truth." She wiped the remaining tears from her cheeks. "Ms. Martin, you can rest assured that I will help you accomplish these goals. Let me give you my card and-." I was stopped in midsentence by the interruption of my ringing cell phone. "Excuse me for just a second," I said before taking the call.

"Listen, I really have to go," I said with my hand over the phone. "I'll be in touch," I finished. I grabbed the paperwork from the table and stuffed it inside the envelope before rushing out the door to the crime scene that I had just been informed about.

Once I was inside my car, I quickly stuffed the information I had just obtained from my new client inside the pocket of my briefcase. I had planned to review it later. Right now, all I could concentrate on was my destination. Although I wasn't looking forward to seeing the seven-year-old boy's lifeless body sprawled out on the floor of his abductor's apartment, I was ecstatic about finally catching the son of a bitch who had gotten away with this crime twice before. My blood boiled as I approached Blueridge Apartments. All I could think about was my own children and the things I would do had this crime happened to one of them. The thought alone made me weak all over.

THIRTY – FIVE – VICTOR

I sat in my car outside of the hotel waiting for my wife to come out. I started thinking about the way I had treated her over the years and I had to admit that I slightly felt like shit. I still felt a tremendous amount of rage for what she was doing and there was no telling what I was going to do to her once we were finally face-to-face but I felt remorseful for the years of hell I put her through. She was a good woman in the wrong place at the wrong time. She deserved none of the things that I did to her, hell no human being did. I can recall one time when I messed her up pretty badly. She resembled something from a horror movie when I had finished with her. I was sure that if she had left the house any that week, I would have been spending the rest of my life behind bars.

We were at a family member's house for a cookout one Sunday afternoon. I was out back enjoying some drinks and a card game with a few of my uncles and cousins. It was normally where all of the males in the family ended up after we got our bellies full. The women usually disappeared into the kitchen to clean up or sit around and chat with one another.

I had beat everyone in the last couple of rounds and some of my cousins were starting to take it a little personal. My little cousin Tad was especially irritated with my back to back wins. "Aw come on Taddy Tad," I said trying to sound as though I was feeling sorry for him. "The best man won. Don't be a hater," I said smiling. When his facial expression didn't change I knew that the alcohol was probably getting to him and that it was probably a good time to get my wife and go. "Alright y'all," I said reaching over to give my decent acting family members a goodbye handshake. "I bet you weren't the damn best man the other night when I saw your old lady with Tank on the passenger side of her car," Tad said. Now he was the one smiling while I sat embarrassed and infuriated. Embarrassment was an emotion that I didn't deal with too well. Even though I knew deep down inside that my wife wouldn't touch Tank with a fifty-foot pole, I still wanted to find her and knock the shit out of her for doing something so foolish. "Say what," I said. "Yeah, I bet you wiped that damn Kool-Aid ass grin off of your face now," he said laughing. I wanted to punch a hole right through him. I could feel my jaws and fists clenching. He had just delivered a low blow and I couldn't believe it had all started with a card game.

In the house, I could hear the laughter of my wife, mom, grandmother and other family members. "You ready?" I asked with a blank look on my face. She looked around before responding as if she knew something was wrong. "Just let me get my jacket," she said nervously. After I kissed my mom and grandmother on the cheek, I stormed out of the house. Once inside the car I wasted no time confronting her about what Tad had just told me. "It wasn't even like that," she said. "It was that week when Paula was getting the starter put on her car and he needed a ride to work. I took him to work that one day and told him he would have to find other means the rest of the week." She looked terrified. "So you thought that it would be fine with me if you only took him one day? So is that how you think? Is it okay to do anything as long as you do it one time only?" She frowned and shook her head repeatedly in response to my questions. "You fucked him, didn't you?"

Her facial expression told me that she knew how this night was going to end. "What?" Tears started to run down her face but that didn't faze me one bit. I backed out of the driveway and started driving like a bat out of hell. All I wanted to do was get her home and show her just how fucked up her actions were.

Once we had gotten in the house, she begged to call Tank. She wanted him to confirm that my accusations were ridiculous. She managed to dial a few numbers before I took the phone and threw it up against the wall. I walked towards her and grabbed her by the neck. "I don't want to hear anything from the dude that has been fucking my wife. You must really be trying to play me for a fool." Her eyes looked helpless as she stared at me. They looked like they were seconds away from popping out of her head. I decided to loosen my grip on her neck and started pounding her face for what felt like minutes. I couldn't care less what she would look like in the morning.

Finally, I reached a level of satisfaction when I saw blood coming from her mouth. I figured it was time to stop the beating at that point. She was almost unrecognizable and I knew that she would have some serious swelling in the morning. This would prevent her from going into work for more than a couple of days.

I decided not to wait to apologize. I immediately let her know how sorry I was like the men in the movies did. I always wondered how men could beat their wives then show remorse the moment the beating was over with. They would literally be down on their knees seconds later, telling them how sorry they were. "Baby, listen. I know I have a problem. I'm willing to get counseling if that's what it takes. Just please don't leave me," I begged. She pulled away at first but it wasn't long before the frowns in her face softened and she forgave me. Tears flowed down her face as I pulled her towards me. Just like many times before, I told her that I was sorry and that it would never happen again.

THIRTY – SIX – ANGELICA

"Seriously! So you're really just gonna pull out in front of me going ten damn miles an hour?" I yelled at the driver in front of me who was driving the rusted green station wagon. He proceeded to drive slowly as if he had no idea that I was even there. I had been trying to work on my road rage lately but it was a slow process. It was either work on my anger behind the wheel or move my ass out of the entire state of Maryland. The people around here can't drive for shit and it only got worse when it rained. For the most part, I had gotten a lot better with it but situations like this set me all the way back. The self-help CD that I had purchased coached me into becoming a more patient driver and also helped me to realize what was triggering the road rage in the first place. It turns out that not being on time usually brought on episodes of driving ridiculously as well as cursing and screaming at drivers from the top of my lungs.

When I pulled into the restaurant parking lot, I could clearly see that there were no parking spaces available. Without any time to waste, I parked in the back of the restaurant and entered the building through the back entrance. "Lord, please don't let me have to curse this lady out. If she's in the same kind of mood she was in this morning, I know she's pretty bitchy right about now," I said. Once I made it inside the restaurant, I was greeted by a hostess who led me to the table that was occupied by the PI just a few minutes before I arrived. As the gothic looking waitress ran off to stop my future business partner, I took a moment to breath and woosah for the first time since I got out of bed.

I was on the verge of catching a serious headache from all the stressing and running around that I had done throughout day. I was praying that the PI wouldn't add to my problems. I knew that she didn't play when it came to wasting her time. Ayslan told me about the time when she had arrived a few minutes after her scheduled appointment time. Miss PI had waited around just to inform her that she had to reschedule but only after she had paid her for that day's meeting, a meeting that wouldn't even take place.

Within seconds, the waitress had returned and she was accompanied by one of the most beautiful women that I had ever seen. I stared at her, admiring everything from her face to her physique. I had a flashback of what I thought she looked like when we spoke over the phone. I imagined her to be at least fifty-pounds overweight. That was my fault for assuming that she had an obsession with donuts and coffee. I also pictured her wearing an oversized black business suit with an old scuffed up pair of flat penny loafers. I couldn't have been more wrong about the beauty queen who stood before me. This woman was the complete opposite. She had a slim frame and curves that would catch the attention of any man. She wore the baddest blue and white pinstriped suit and a pair of stilettos that matched perfectly. I could tell that she had expensive taste because I had the exact same pair of shoes. They were a gift from Bryson for our five-year anniversary. She extended her hand towards me and I noticed the beautiful rock on her finger. "Her man must really be something special. She'd better keep him close," I thought to myself. I looked up at her and into her big bright brown eyes. She was so beautiful that I became a little envious. She seemed to have it all; the career, a man who obviously spoiled her and beauty. I tried to convince myself that her brown eyes and long curly hair had to be artificial. At least that's what I wanted to believe.

After a very brief introduction, she asked me to tell her exactly why I needed her services. Once I was finished, she took the liberty of enlightening me on just how good of a private investigator she was. "Ms. Martin, you can rest assured that I will help you to accomplish your goals. As you've requested, I will have all the pertinent information and you can proceed with it as you wish. I just want to advise you that these things can sometimes get messy." She looked around to scan the room. "You don't know what he's told her and what she has chosen to believe, so tread lightly." She stared at me with a look of compassion.

"Let me give you my card and-," she was stopped in midsentence by the ringing of her cell phone. The call must have been an emergency because she ended our meeting. She informed me that she would be in touch before quickly grabbing my paperwork and rushing out the door. I sat alone at the table, anticipating the results of her research.

THIRTY – SEVEN – PEYTON

"What do we have so far besides the obvious?" I asked the police officer who had been the first on the scene. He informed me that the suspect was a thirty-six-year-old male who had a history of mental illness. He even mentioned to me that the sick, twisted son of a bitch was convicted of raping one of his own sisters a couple of years prior.

"So please enlighten me on the reason why he was never required to register as a sex offender," I asked angrily. "I'm not sure ma'am. I was told by officer Hyman that he somehow talked his way out of it. Rumor has it, he's a very clever individual," he informed. "Clever my ass," I said under my breath as I walked over to the police car that was occupied by the suspect. I wanted to have a few words with him and what I had to say couldn't wait until we got back to the station. "Detective Hainesworth." I could hear my lieutenant call me from the entrance of the apartment. I turned around to find him signaling for me to come inside. "Motherfucker better consider himself lucky. Maybe by the time he had to see me, I would have calmed down just a little bit," I thought.

Once inside, I was instructed by my lieutenant to take a

look at the master bedroom. When I arrived at the last room down the dark hallway, I couldn't believe my eyes. There were at least fifteen photographs of young boys hanging on the walls throughout the room. I noticed that one of the pictures was that of the deceased boy who was just carried out in a body bag. I shook my head at the thought of the sick bastard raping children. I also took the opportunity to thank God for him being caught so that he would never get the chance to do this to the other boys whose pictures were lined up on his roach infested wall. The only thing I wanted to do at that point was get back over to the station so that I could be there waiting for him when he arrived but first I had to make my way over to the home of Travis Donavan. I had to deliver the news that no parent should ever have to hear.

They had been diligent in the search to find their son. Even long after our crews had left for the day, they continued with flashlights and their faith in God. I had never seen so much dedication in all my years on the force. I dreaded the moment that I would look into their eyes and watch them fall apart. Informing the family had to be the hardest part of my job but it had to be done.

After instructing one of the police officers on the scene to find me the address of the victim's family, I went back to my car to get myself together. This day had been too much for me and I was mentally and physically drained. All I wanted to do was sit in my bathtub with a glass of wine, matter-of-fact, make that the whole bottle. First it was the meeting with my new client, who had shown up late. "Speaking of which, let me see what we're dealing with here," I said aloud while rummaging through my briefcase.

Once I located the manila envelope, I opened it and skimmed through the information that she provided. "I am so happy that this is going to be my last P.I. case," I said to myself while shaking my head. I had enjoyed my time as a PI but it was time to stop spending my free time chasing clues and cracking cases. I was so thankful that Bryson was going to be able to take care of me the way he once had. I was looking forward to him spoiling me for a change.

I studied the top portion of the application and felt a sense of sadness. This woman had gotten herself into some mess and there was nothing that she could do about it. Out of feeling desperate and helpless, she had decided to retaliate in the worst way by reaching out to his wife. I tried to advise her, without getting too involved, that she should be careful when approaching the other woman. I was willing to provide her with any information that I could obtain because it was my job but I didn't agree with the way she had chosen to go about things.

Most of my clients hired me because they wanted to know if their significant other was cheating on them. In her case, she already had that information. She just wanted to find his wife to inflict the same pain onto her that he had caused her to endure. I don't know what I'd do if someone had called me up and told me that she had been sleeping with my husband. I don't even want to think about my reaction to her having a whole ten-year-old child.

The top portion of the application was reserved for all of the accuser's basic information, such as their occupation and address along with a description of the accused. She had listed his eye color, height, texture of his hair and the type of car he drove. I made my way down to the bottom half of the sheet of paper where she had listed the accused's name. Suddenly, the paper became heavier than a ton of bricks. I scanned over the first line for a second time just to see if my eyes were playing tricks on me. "Name of the accused," I read. "Bryson Hainesworth." I placed my hand over my mouth in shock as I craved for clarity of the situation. "This can't be right. There has to be a reasonable explanation for this," I tried to convince myself. I tried hard to make sense of what I had just read.

Once I was able to remove my hand from my mouth, I

reached deep down into the envelope for the photograph Ms. Martin had provided. With the picture in my hands, I closed my eyes and said a short prayer. I practically begged God for this to be some kind of mistake and that this Bryson Hainesworth was not the same man that I had been married to for the past eighteen years. When I opened my eyes, I turned over the picture that I had been gripping tightly between my sweaty fingers and revealed the person in the picture.

THIRTY – EIGHT – FRANKIE

I felt helpless sitting in one spot doing nothing but feeling sorry for myself. I felt like I needed to be brainstorming, trying to figure out my next move. I laid back on my hotel room bed and cupped my hands behind my head. She really didn't mean the things she said about us, about him. I knew her better than anyone and I was certain that her heart was with me. I saw it in her face the night of the party and the night that we were together. I could even tell by the way her juices flowed down and the way her body trembled when I touched her. I couldn't be fooled the way she had managed to fool everyone else. I knew better and I wanted to tell her exactly how I felt.

I contemplated paying her a visit at the station where she worked but I knew that would probably piss her off more than anything. I even considered sitting outside of her house and waiting for Bryson to leave before showing up at her door. Something about that seemed too risky since there were two teenagers that I had to also try to dodge.

Finally, I had come up with a plan. I reached into the trash can to grab the card that I had thrown away the night before. I had crumbled it up since I had no intentions of using it. The card had been given to me at the party. While I was standing by the bar with a group of Peyton's coworkers, one of them slid the card into my pocket. Since I wasn't attracted to the flirty coworker at all and had no desire of being with anyone besides Peyton, I crumbled it up and threw it away once I got to my room. I had no idea that it would come in handy and help me get closer to the woman I loved.

I dialed the ten digits and anxiously waited for an answer. The soft voice of a young lady greeted me and asked how she could help. After I asked for Detective Hainesworth, she politely told me she wasn't in the office and that she would be more than happy to give me her voicemail. I could instantly tell that I was dealing with someone that was gullible and that getting Peyton's number would be a simple challenge if I played my cards right. "I have some information that she requested about her latest case. She told me to call her A.S.A.P. in the event that I found anything," I lied. Trying hard not to sound desperate, I offered to call her back later. I knew this would be the key to the door I was trying to open. Just like I figured, she stopped me from hanging up the phone and offered to give me Peyton's cell phone number. It seemed way too easy. I was grinning like a Cheshire cat as she read each of the ten digits. I was starting to feel like I wouldn't be leaving this town empty handed.

As soon as I hung up from the operator, I called Peyton's cell phone. She answered on the second ring, oblivious of the fact that it was me on the other end. She sounded as if she had been crying which tore my heart to pieces. Ever since we were younger I felt the need to protect her and her feelings. Hearing her cry was like hearing my mother cry, it just did something to me. I felt the need to comfort her and find out what in the hell was going on. I quickly learned that some things never changed. She played the stubborn game just like she used to long ago. I asked her if she was alright and she tried to convince me that she was. I wasn't buying it.

When I tried to convince her to come visit me at the hotel, she refused. I just had to see her and I wasn't leaving this town until I was given that opportunity. I provided her with the name and room number of my hotel in hopes that she would change her mind. Finally, she agreed.

THIRTY – NINE – BRYSON

I couldn't remember the last time I had been so eager to get home to my wife. She had been the subject of my thoughts lately the same way she had when we first met. I can remember back in the day when she would come over to visit and I would beg her to stay. I used to crave her presence. I'm amazed that she stuck beside me these past few years because there were so many times when I would push away. I don't know what made her stay. Even I would've left me. Things are different now. Peyton was my number one and all I wanted to do was be with her and only her. I was starting to feel for her the way I felt for Angelica years ago. I had that new feeling, the feeling you get when you're with a brand new person. I wanted that feeling to last and I vowed to never look outside of my marriage for it again.

I had paid Jessica and Bryson Jr. off in exchange for some alone time with their mother. They were going to be staying at my sister's house which has never been an issue since she was roughly ten years older than them. I didn't mind paying the fifty bucks to each of them, including my sister, because having the opportunity to spend time with

Peyton would be all worth it. It had been too long since we had spent any time together and I was looking forward to a night with just the two of us. Plus, I needed to make up for the quick birthday sex that I had given her. I knew that she had been disappointed but she felt so amazing that I couldn't hold back. I could tell that she was just as ready for me as I had been for her. She felt like silk the moment I slipped inside of her which made me lose control sooner than I had planned. It was time for me to start putting her needs first as I once had. I needed to start wining and dining her the way she deserved.

A wise man once told me that just because the numbers on your marriage certificate become old doesn't mean that the marriage has to. That wise man was my father. He and my mother had been married for over fifty years and they were the epitome of what a successful, black marriage should be. He said that you get to the golden years by doing things the way you had in the beginning. He always liked to quote "if you do what you've always done, you'll get what you've always gotten". This phrase usually had a negative connotation but in the case of marriage, it's looked at as a positive statement.

I had already started thinking about having date nights and weekend getaways. I wanted to get back to treating her the way I used to. Tonight I stopped to pick up a bottle of her favorite wine along with a bouquet of her favorite flowers. I needed to make this night a special one for her.

Just as I turned up the smooth sounds of Teddy Pendergrass, I felt the vibration of my cell phone on my hip. "Hello," I answered after noticing that it was Peyton. "Hello," I said again with no response. "I told her to switch from that cheap ass phone company." I smiled and shook my head while returning the phone back to my clip. Without giving the phone call any more thought, I turned the music back up and proceeded to drive home. I was sure that if it was important she would call back.

"Where the hell could she be?" I asked aloud while checking my watch for the time. It was now seven o'clock and I expected Peyton an hour and a half ago. I was starting to get worried. I thought about the phone call earlier and how she had lost her signal. I knew that by now she had to have been in a place that had better reception. A million thoughts started running through my head. I wondered if she was in trouble and that maybe she was trying to call me for help, or maybe she was having car trouble and her phone battery was dying. I worried myself by considering the worst of possibilities. I felt helpless staying in one spot while my wife was God knows where.

I sat with my head held low, thinking about how she must have felt all of those nights when I stood her up. She must have been furious all the times I would ignore her phone calls and then tell her hours later that I was in a meeting that ran over. I felt like shit and I had made my mind up right then and there. If I was ever given the chance, my wife would never have to worry about me or my whereabouts again. "This shit hits different when the shoe is on the other foot," I said to myself.

A few hours of waiting up for my wife and a few phone calls to the nearby hospitals later, I decided to lay on the couch and wait for her. I tried to put my mind at ease by dismissing her lateness as her pulling an all-nighter at the office. I guess I had forgotten about the many nights she would come in late due to work. It had been so long since I'd actually been here to witness what time she would come in. I smiled at the thought of my wife sitting at her desk with her granny glasses pressed down on her small button nose. I called her one last time before drifting off to sleep.

FORTY – VICTOR

I had been sitting in my car for about an hour and there was no sign of her. Her car was still parked where she left it last night but she was nowhere to be found. I was starting to worry because it was never like her to sleep in. Even on the weekends she was up at the crack of dawn looking for something to do. It had been almost an hour and a half since I had been waiting for her and I was getting restless. I pulled out my laptop and decided to read up on today's news back at home.

Today's cover story was about a man who sexually assaulted his girlfriend. He was facing up to fifteen years in prison if convicted but his lawyers were arguing that the sex was consensual. The case got me to thinking because it wasn't that long ago when I was involved in a similar matter.

"Because of the amount of damage done to your body, there should be no sex for at least six weeks," the doctor said before handing over a prescription for Valium. Since she hadn't really been in the mood lately because of the pregnancy, I was sure that this was music to her ears. I knew immediately that this was going to be a problem for me. I was a man with needs and six weeks sounded more like an eternity.

When we arrived at home, she was in a cynical mood. She had blamed the world for the loss of our baby and I had done my best to put up with it. Even though the doctor had told us that she has a condition called of uterine septum which is known to cause frequent miscarriages, she still blamed herself, me and every other woman on the face of the earth that had given birth at some point or another. It was sad watching her go through what seemed to be the most difficult time of her life but it was time she got over it.

It had been a few days since she miscarried and she was feeling better physically. She was up cleaning and back her normal activities. It was week three of the six week healing process and I was horny as hell. I had endured two weeks of pleasing myself and I craved the feeling of being inside of my wife. My hand was no match for her natural juices. After I got out of the shower, I found her sleeping peacefully in our bed covered in a pair of cotton pajamas. She had started wearing them ever since she came home from the hospital and I was starting to think that she was trying to keep me away.

I spooned her and wrapped my arm around her. After a few seconds, I slipped my hand under her shirt and found her plump breasts. She squirmed as if she was uncomfortable but I pretended not to notice. She reached up to pull her shirt down while I took the opportunity to reach my hand into her pants. I found her middle and started trying to finger her. She squeezed her legs together tightly and calmly reminded me that she couldn't engage in sexual activities. I was angry. She was trying to make me suffer for as long as I would allow it and the thought alone infuriated me. I sat up in bed and stared at her for a few seconds before trying to rip off her pants. She started working against me and it became a game of tug of war that I wasn't about to lose. She started to cry as she begged me to understand. I blacked out at some point and my only mission was to take what was already mine in the first place. I focused my attention on her shirt. I snatched it open so hard that I could hear the buttons pop off. She lay naked on the bed with tears running down her face. She stared at me with pure hatred. I could tell that she would rather have been anywhere else in the world than here with me. I tried my best to ignore the expression on her face. It was something that has always been able to turn me off faster than anything else. I felt my once fully erect penis start to turn soft. I quickly forced myself inside of her and got to work.

Once inside of her, I pumped harder. I could tell that she was in pain because the deeper I dug inside of her, the louder her sobs were, but I didn't care. There was only one thing on my mind and that was getting mine.

When it was all over I fell weakly on top of her. Almost immediately I realized that what I had done was wrong. I had forced myself on my wife and I wasn't sure what she was going to do about it. I didn't know enough about the law to determine whether or not I had just committed a crime. The unknown terrified me and I knew I had to do something to make things right before business hours. I lifted myself off of her and proceeded to go back to the spooning position. I wrapped my arms around her and started mentally preparing my apology.

I truly was sorry but when she threw my arm off of her, I had a change of heart. I quickly and tightly grabbed her arm and pressed my lips against her ear. "Don't you ever try that shit again. I own you and that will never ever change. If I ever even think you're thinking about leaving me," I paused before finishing. "I'll kill you," I finished.

The compassion I felt for the woman on the news surprised me. I was even pissed with the lawyers for trying to plead the case that the act of forcing himself on his wife was consensual. I imagined my wife's face the night she lay under me helplessly. I can't imagine what was going through her mind while she was unable to move because she was being held down by a body that weighed twice as much as she had.

I rubbed my hands over my face to keep from allowing my emotions to get out of control. When I looked back up, I saw my wife walking towards her car. She was walking out of the hotel carrying her suitcase and a couple of overnight bags. She looked more beautiful than I had remembered.

FORTY – ONE – PEYTON

"Hello," I answered in a raspy voice. "Hello. Are you alright?" asked the voice on the other end. "Yes. Who's speaking," I cleared my throat. "It's Frankie. Are you sure everything's okay?" I couldn't believe my ears. "How did you get this number?" I snapped. "Please, Peyton. I called your office and the switchboard operator gave it to me after I convinced her that I had some important information about a case. Please don't hang up."

I couldn't speak. I didn't know what to say. I wasn't sure if I wanted to continue the conversation or end the call. The last thing I wanted to do was complicate things even further but I was vulnerable right now. I was desperate for conversation and Frankie had always been a good listener. Back in the day, there was no one else I would even consider calling whenever I would have a problem. I would dial Frankie's number, lay out my problems and they would disappear by the end of the call. I needed a listening ear. The information that I had received minutes ago was enough to make me proceed with the conversation. I needed someone to talk to, and at this point, Frankie would just have to do. I had made an attempt to contact Bryson but decided hang up the phone after a couple of rings. I didn't want to discuss the matter over the phone. My father always said 'things are better said in person. Folks will hardly lie to your face, but over the phone, that's a different case.

"What is it Frankie?" I asked. "I want to see you, and judging by the sound of your voice, I need to see you." There was a pause. "I leave tomorrow and I would love to see you before I go. Please meet me at my hotel. I'm staying at the Bluebay Suites. I'll let the front desk know that you're coming. I'm in room four-forty-two." I wasn't sure how to respond. I knew that I wasn't thinking rationally but I was hurt. I felt like my heart had been ripped from my chest and I knew that Frankie had the ability to ease the pain that I was feeling. Even if only temporary, I needed some relief from the ultimate hurt. "Okay," I said before ending the call.

I started having second thoughts as soon as I pulled into the parking lot. A million thoughts were running through my head and the one that I dismissed the most was the one that was trying to tell me that it wasn't too late to turn around. I was experiencing an extreme case of devil versus angel and they were having a nasty fight on my shoulders. I still hadn't gotten over the guilt from our rendezvous. It's funny how women can get dogged out and still feel guilty for the little bit that we do. My husband has been living a double life for the past decade and I was the one feeling guilty. I still couldn't believe that he thought he could just send the woman and her child away and pick up where he left off with me. The devil fucking wins. I plan to fuck Frankie's brains out tonight.

When I entered the suite, I was welcomed with a kiss so passionate I could feel my panties become moist. It almost knocked me off of my feet. We stumbled towards to couch, never once unlocking our lips. Frankie removed my heels and propped my feet up on the glass coffee table. Somehow between kisses and massages, our clothes were removed. We were now both naked from head to toe and I was enjoying the view.

We made our way to the bedroom and that's where I found a king size bed covered with red roses. A small white envelope was neatly placed in the center of the bed. "You did all of this for me?" I asked while looking in Frankie's direction. I smiled for the first time since I received the heartbreaking news about Bryson. "Of course I did. There has never been anything I wouldn't do for you, and there is still nothing that I wouldn't do for you. I smiled shyly before I crawled sexily on top of the oversized bed and grabbed the envelope. I laid there sprawled on the bed, looking Frankie up and down. I admired the beautiful body that hadn't changed much since we were committed lovers almost two decades earlier.

"Come here," I said as I used my index finger to signal for Frankie to join me in the bed. I tossed the envelope to the side. The look in those big brown eyes told me that my changed behavior had come as a total shock. After Frankie was positioned comfortably on the bed, I made the selfless decision to return the favor that was done for me the other night. I kissed my way down Frankie's body and began pleasing the center like I had never done before.

"Yeah baby," Frankie said which made me want to lick and suck harder. All of the excitement had made me just a little jealous. I then climbed on top of Frankie and positioned myself in the six-nine position. This always heated things up between the two of us back in the day. After pleasing each other orally, I crawled down and laid flat on the bed. I spread my legs apart for easier access and allowed Frankie to slide inside of me. Sounds of pleasure filled the room before we kissed passionately and fell asleep in each other's arms.

FORTY – TWO – FRANKIE

I had been sitting on the edge of the bed for quite some time going over what I wanted to say to her before she left this morning. I could feel her start to squirm uncomfortably before she finally got out of bed. I watched her naked body as she moved gracefully across the room. As badly as I wanted to grab her and bring her back to bed, I decided that letting her go was for the best. I wasn't sure if I was prepared for the rejection that awaited me. I knew it was coming because I was already familiar with how this worked. We have the most amazing time only for her to come to her senses and tell me how much of a mistake that it was. I wanted to hold onto this moment. I knew that confronting her could possibly damage what happiness I still had. I watched as she quickly threw on her clothes and gathered her shoes from the floor. She didn't speak and neither did I. We didn't have to because we knew what each other was thinking. I didn't want to hear the excuses and she didn't want to hear me beg her stay. She grabbed her keys and overnight bag and she was gone.

I was left alone, just like always. Once again, we had an amazing night together and once again, I got nowhere. I still hadn't convinced her that she should be with me. I was starting to come to terms with the fact that I may actually leave this town empty handed. I wondered if she left this morning because she had to get home and get ready for work or if the guilt had once again become too much for her. I had to consider the fact that she may never admit that we were meant to be together. She had created this new life for herself and there may just be no space for me in it. I couldn't believe my plan had failed. I was running out of ideas and was struggling to accept the fact that my life may have to go on without her. Maybe she was happy. Maybe she was with the person she truly wanted to be with. The best thing for me to do might be to pack my shit and go back to my life at home. Although I wasn't happy with the way things turned out for me here, I was willing to go home and make the necessary changes in order for me to be happy. I actually had some spring cleaning of my own to do and there was no better time to do it then now.

After I finally mustered the strength to get out of bed, I went into the kitchen to make a cup of coffee. I was exhausted from the past 24 hours and I was hoping that it would give me even the slightest bit of energy. I felt like I had the weight of the world on my shoulders. There was nothing left that I could possibly say to Peyton that would change her mind about being with me. She had gotten over us and now it was time that I did as well.

The coffee provided temporary relief but it did the trick. After I showered, I made the decision to visit some old friends whom I hadn't seen in a while. Since checkout was just a couple of hours away, I decided to go ahead and pack my bags. That way I wouldn't have to make an unnecessary trip back. When I arrived at the front desk to turn in my key, I looked to my right and saw a familiar face. "Could this be who I think it is?" I asked myself. After a few more glances, I had determined that it was a rather rough version of the lover boy himself. He looked like death itself with his red eyes and wrinkled clothing. I imagined that it would be safe to assume that he had been up all night wondering where his wife was. Even though I still didn't know for sure what was going on with Peyton and her melancholy mood over the phone the day before, I was starting to feel like it had something to do with the unpleasant sight that stood before me. I listened as he gave his information and I wondered why in the hell he was planning to stay at a hotel for a week. I tried hard to mind my own business so I retrieved my receipt and went on with my day. Peyton or her husband were no longer my problem and it was time for me to move on.

FORTY – THREE – BRYSON

I woke up on the couch around seven-thirty to a throbbing pressure in my bladder that demanded my attention. As I made my way to the bathroom, I hoped that I would peak in the bedroom and find my wife sleeping peacefully. I was wrong. There was still no sign of her and I had lost all hope that this was just one of her long days turned late nights. This was more than just her losing track of time and dozing off at the office. Something wasn't right. It had been hours since I last heard from her and I was getting frustrated at this point. I picked up the phone to see if she had called throughout the night only to find that she hadn't. I'd had enough. I grabbed the shirt I had worn the night before and threw on my shoes before heading out the door.

"Damn," I thought to myself as I stared into the eyes of my weekly Jehovah's witness visitor. She looked as surprise as I was that I had actually opened the door for her. "Hello. Do you mind if we come in for a minute and talk to you about the world and how we could all make it a better place before it's too late?" She smiled at me before nodding towards the car parked outside of my yard. Her partner must have known that I wasn't going to give them any of my time.

She just waved and decided to stay in the car. "No thank you. Could you come back another time, preferably in the evenings when my wife is home." I often times put unwanted visitors or telemarketers on Peyton. She was so much better at getting rid of them than I was. Peyton always said that I carried on too much conversation with them instead of just getting to the point. It annoyed her so much that she would take the phone from me and tell them that we weren't interested. I could really use her help right about now.

"Okay but may I just leave you some reading material?" she asked while trying to force two thin pamphlets into my hands. "No thank you. Look, I really have to go," I said before locking and closing my front door and practically making a run for it towards my truck. She was left standing on my front porch alone.

As soon as I backed out of the driveway, I looked in my rear view mirror and saw that Peyton's silver Chevy Equinox was coming up the street behind me. "Well, well, damn it well," I mumbled. I stayed where I was in order to allow her to pull into the driveway.

After she got out of the car, she stood in the driveway and made eye contact with the unwanted visitors. They must've thought they had perfect timing because the middle aged woman made her way back up to the house. My wife's words stopped her dead in her tracks. "Lady, before you waste your time and breath, let me just inform you that I am not in the mood to talk about the end of the world or whatever other madness you've predicted is going to happen soon. Now you can just keep your little pamphlets because I am not interested and will never be interested in becoming a Jehovah's witness." The look on the woman's face was priceless. "Thank you for your time ma'am. Have a good day," the petite lady hurried back to her car. I took one look at Peyton and I knew that something was wrong. The big question in my mind was, what the hell could it be.

Once we were both inside the house, I wasted no time trying to figure out what was going on. She stared at me from across the room. Her arms were folded and she appeared to be upset with me. I couldn't understand how she had the audacity to give me attitude when she was the one who stayed out all night without so much as a phone call to let me know that she was safe. "You do realize that it's after eight in the morning and you didn't come home last night, right?" I asked. "Sit down Bryson," she said calmly. "What?" I asked. "Sit the fuck down!" she shouted angrily.

I wasn't sure where this was going so I just sat my black ass down. My wife was obviously pissed as hell and all I could focus on was the three-fifty-seven that she wore on her waist. She threw her brief case on the glass kitchen table and proceeded to open it. I was still unsure where all this was going. She took some paper from the case along with a manila envelope and threw them on the table before me. I looked up at her confused.

"Bryson, I want you to take a look at the paperwork that lies before you and tell me exactly what your findings are," she said in a calm voice that seemed forced. I wasted no time picking up the paperwork and immediately I knew exactly what this was. It was one of the applications her clients completed after requesting a private investigation. I still wasn't sure what this had to do with me, that is until I decided to open up the envelope. "Ah shit," I thought while looking at the photo of me, my mistress, and my son, Bryson Jr. My heart fell into my hands as I feared looking up at my wife. "Peyton, look I can explain," I begged. "Explain what?" she said. "Explain to me why this woman claims to have shared not only a home with you for the past ten years, but also a son," she said. "How could you? How could you do this to me?" she screamed.

"Peyton, just calm down," I tried to console her by putting my hands on her arms. "Let go of me you fucking bastard! Don't you fucking touch me!" she screamed. "Now I know where you were all those times you said you had conferences out of town. You were right around the corner from me and I didn't have a clue. How could I have been so stupid to fall for this shit?" she said through sobs. I walked over to her in an attempt to try and explain myself once again. "Peyton, please, you have to believe me. She means nothing-," I was cut off in midsentence. "Save it for my lawyer Bryson. There is nothing you can say to me. You can't lie your way out of this one."

Her tone became softer. "I gave you my all and you took it for granted. How could you sleep at night? And all that bullshit about you wanting to marry me again." She shook her head before leaving the room. She left me with my tail between my legs wondering how in the hell I was going to fix the mess I had gotten myself into.

FORTY – FOUR – ANGELICA

After informing my sister of my new relationship status, she practically begged me to let her give Jeremy my number. There was no doubt that I was attracted to him physically but I wasn't ready for anything serious. After what I had been through with Bryson, I had some serious healing to do before I could even think about giving my heart away again. "Girl I'm not asking to plan your wedding, just to give you the hook up, that's all," she said.

There was a part of me that looked at Jeremy coming into my life as perfect timing. On the other hand, I was starting to feel like all men were dogs. They all seemed perfect in the beginning. Who's to say he wasn't going to play me the same way Bryson had? The thought alone made me angry but I also didn't want to miss out on a good thing, if that's what this was.

Within the same five minutes of my sister getting off the phone with me, I received a phone call from him. "Damn. Brother didn't waste any time," I said aloud before picking up the phone as I read Jeremy Cooley on the caller ID. "So, is it alright if I come see you before I go to work this afternoon?" he asked. "Jeremy, it's just that I'm not sure if

I'm ready for another-," he cut me off before I had the chance to finish. "Angelica, there are no strings attached. I just want to see you, that's all. Maybe bring you some lunch. You have to eat, don't you?" he asked. "Okay, now you're talking. I'll take "the China sampler" from A Taste of China, please," I said. "Yeah, I knew that would change your mind. Ayslan told me the way to your heart was through your stomach," he joked. I laughed. "I can't believe she told you that. I'm definitely going to kill her," I said. "Well, I'll see you around eleven," he said. "Eleven," I confirmed.

After I got out of the shower, I decided to spruce up a little bit for my guest. I made my way to the living room after hearing a knock at the door. "Wow, I could get use to a man that is on time," I said to myself. Without looking out the window, I opened the door. Staring me in the face was not exactly the person I was expecting, instead, it was Bryson. "What are you doing here?" I asked. He looked a mess. His face looked like he had been crying and his wrinkled clothes looked as though he had slept in them. As I looked him up and down, there was a part of me that wanted to laugh. It was always pleasurable when I would see an old boyfriend down on his luck after breaking my heart.

He invited himself in as he brushed past me. He sat on the couch and gave me the most hateful stare. "How could you do this to me?" he asked in a cracked voice. "You just couldn't accept the fact that I no longer wanted you so you had to go and ruin my happy home as well," he cried. "Bryson, what are you talking about?" I asked. I was confused since I hadn't told anyone the details of Bryson's secret life. There was no way anyone could have known about his wife.

"I'm talking about you going to my wife. You just couldn't rest without fucking up my life, could you?" He walked closer to me and then he grabbed my arms. "You know what?" he said in a low unpleasant voice. "All you ever were was my whore." He paused before finishing.

"And that's all you will ever be," he said while squeezing my arms and shaking my entire body. "Let go of me!" I demanded. "You have it all wrong you two-timing bastard," I said while snatching away from his grip. "You deserve every bad thing that's coming your way. My only wish is that you rot in hell," I said while pointing my finger at him.

He plopped down on the couch and threw his hands in the air. He chuckled sarcastically. "If only I wasn't busy taking care of your stupid ass," he said. I wasn't sure what made Bryson think that I went to his wife. The private investigator was supposed to find the necessary information needed for me to locate her but she was never supposed to have any contact with her. Either way, my work was done. I got revenge without even having to lift a finger or a phone for that matter.

I got nothing but pure pleasure watching the man who broke my heart sit helplessly before me. I believed he deserved everything that came his way as a result of his lies. I needed him to feel a portion of the pain he had caused me. I was the one who was left alone to take care of our child. Even after considering all of these things, I still felt a little sorry for him. Boy, if Dina ever heard me say that aloud, she would ask me if I had lost my damn mind.

"Bryson, you need to go," I said. "What? I don't have to do a damn thing. Bitch, this is all of my shit up in here. Even the damn toilet paper you wipe your ass with was bought with my money," he said. I contemplated slapping the shit out of him for calling me a bitch but I dismissed it when I thought about how happy the private investigator had just made me. There was nothing Bryson could say or do to steal my joy. I had burned him just as bad as he had burned me and it felt damn good. "Bryson, leave now," I demanded. "And what in the hell are you going to do if I don't?" he asked with a smirk on his face. Before I could respond, there was knock at the door.

FORTY – FIVE – VICTOR

Even though it was obvious that my wife had left me because she could no longer bear being tormented daily, I was still very optimistic that she'd come back to me. It was unlike her to just up and leave and I assumed this time would be no different from the others. She never stayed mad at me long. It would usually only take an apology and a little convincing that I was a changed man for her to forgive me. I knew that this time would be no different if I could just talk to her. "Damn it!" I slapped the steering wheel. I was done with her games. She had played this out much longer than I had expected and it was time for her to stop all the bullshit.

I sat in my car and watched as she drove off. I prayed that she was going to turn into the direction of our hometown. I hadn't prepared for this. I watched her walk out of the hotel with her bags in hand. If she wasn't going home, where the hell was she going? I struggled to jump lanes to follow her. Traffic was bumper to bumper and drivers weren't allowing anyone to squeeze in between. I felt so helpless watching the back of her car get smaller and smaller before it finally vanished down an unknown road. I pulled off the road and into a gas station to gather my thoughts and figure out my next move. I had a million thoughts and a list of unanswered questions running through my mind.

I made the decision to go back to the hotel and pay for another night. I had no idea where she was going, which meant I had no idea how long my stay was going to be. I also needed a place to sort things out and determine what my next move would be. For the remainder of the day I hung out in my hotel and planned to go back out later that afternoon.

I ended up falling asleep. I woke up around four feeling well rested and eager to find my wife. After I got up and threw my clothes back on, I headed out. I found myself riding with no particular place in mind. I had previously checked all of the places I could think of and I had run out of ideas.

I spotted this barbeque place on the side of the road and realized how long it had actually been since I enjoyed a good sandwich packed with extra sauce and cole slaw.

Once inside, I noticed they had a nice little set up with big screen TVs on every wall. I had everything I needed to clear my mind; barbeque, basketball and beer. It couldn't get any better than that.

I spent most of my evening at The Barbeque Bar and Grill before I decided it was time to start heading back. Today was a wasted day but tomorrow would be about finding my wife. I had only taken a couple of days off work and I had to be heading back home with or without her.

After I got back to my hotel I jumped straight in the shower. I wanted nothing more than to wash the strong scent of cigarette smoke off of me. It was the only thing I hated about going to bars. You were bound to leave with every part of your body smelling like a bonfire. Once I had scrubbed down in my favorite body wash and threw on my pajamas, I flipped through the channels for a little while before drifting off to sleep.

Sometime after I had dozed off I heard commotion coming from the room next door to me. It sounded like a couple having an argument but I couldn't make out exactly what they were saying. From what I could hear, it seemed as though the woman was winning and the man was punking out. They were loud as hell and I was surprised that no one had complained about them yet. I was tired but with all of the noise that was coming through the walls, it had become clear to me that I wasn't going to get any sleep. I decided to pull out my laptop. I surfed the internet for nothing in particular while waiting for my obnoxious neighbors to kiss and make up if they didn't kill each other first. Either way would have been fine with me.

All of a sudden I heard another voice come into the mix and I thought how could I be so unlucky tonight. Sounded to me like someone had just gotten caught cheating. As the voices grew louder I grew more and more agitated. I threw on my clothes and found myself standing at the door. With my fist ready to pound on the door, I stood there ready to take action. What I heard next sent me running back to my room faster than a bunny being chased by wolves.

FORTY – SIX – PEYTON

I couldn't help but sit and reflect on all the times Bryson had told me he was working late. Every business meeting that had ran over was a lie. All the times he would claim to be at weekend conventions that would cause him to miss important family events were lies. These had all been sorry ass excuses to be with his other woman and their lovechild. More than half of our marriage has been based on a lie. "Ten years with this woman and I had no clue at all," I thought. I felt like a fool. How could I have allowed him to get away with this all of these years? I was one of the best detectives in the state and I couldn't see that my husband had been living a double life for more than a decade. I wonder how long he would have let this go on had it not been for his baby mama coming to tell me herself. I wanted to know more about the woman who had been sleeping with my husband for the past ten years. I wanted to know every detail of their secret love affair. How often did she see him? What was their sex life like? Did he do things with her that he did with me? Although I knew it wasn't healthy, I felt like I needed to know the whole story. Hell, I deserved to know.

I had decided to sneak out of the room without waking

Frankie. After the night we had, I knew there must be a million questions waiting for me. Truth was, I wasn't sure what I was going to do at this point. I didn't know for sure if I wanted to continue spending the rest of my life with Bryson and I never considered being with Frankie. I had a lot of thinking to do and I sure as hell couldn't do it with Frankie breathing down my neck. I gently rolled out of bed and managed to throw on my clothes and grab my shoes. Within five minutes, I was on the elevator and on the way to my truck.

"Good morning lieutenant. It's Peyton," I greeted him as cheerful as possible. "Morning. Talk to me." he replied. "I'm going to need to take a personal day today, if that's okay." I prayed that he didn't ask the reason why as he normally did. "Well," he sighed. "I think us guys can handle things around here. You take all the time you need," he finished. "Thank you, sir. I'll see you tomorrow," I confirmed.

"Thirty-two-twenty-five Opal Circle," I read aloud the directions to my client's home from her application. I wasn't sure if popping up unannounced was the right thing to do but it was a chance that I was willing to take. I was pretty sure that calling her up with 'I know you know me as the private investigator but I'm actually the woman you're trying to find, you know, your boyfriend's wife' wouldn't be received well. She would probably disconnect the call in disbelief. I finally decided that the best thing for me to do was to show up and have a sit down with her. After all, she had been waiting on the results of the investigation. If not now, she would be calling me soon anyway.

As I turned into the neighborhood where my husband lived with his side-chick, I was blown away by all the beautiful homes. I had passed through the area before but I never would've guessed that this little community even existed. Bryson was smart to pick this spot out. It was the perfect secluded area to hide his side family. "This must be it," I said to myself as I laid eyes on one of the most beautiful homes I had ever seen. I studied the manicured lawn as I pulled into the driveway. I wondered if he took care of the grass, or even worse, if he had hired our lawn guy to maintain both of his homes. I noticed a black Cadillac Escalade parked in the yard. "Either they have matching vehicles or Bryson had decided to pay his little girlfriend a visit after I talked to him this morning," I said aloud.

I contemplated pulling out of the driveway and leaving but decided against it. I wanted nothing more than to see the look on Bryson's face once he realized I was here. I could hear the two of them arguing as I approached the door. Bryson was calling her out her name while she commanded him to leave. "If I wanted to be nasty, I'd march right in there and arrest his ass," I thought to myself.

The arguing stopped the second I knocked at the door. "Please come in," offered my client. I made eye contact with Bryson while watching him placing his hands behind his head nervously. He looked as though he would have rather slit his ass and take an alcohol bath than to have had me find him here. "This is-," Angelica tried to introduce the bastard I was all too familiar with. "You son of a bitch. Did you come here to try and reconcile with your girlfriend?" I asked.

All he could do was bring his hands up to his face, creating a praying motion. "Wait a minute. Do you two know each other?" Angelica asked. Without ever removing my eyes from Bryson, I answered. "Angelica, my name is Peyton Hainesworth and this is my husband, Bryson Hainesworth." There was a moment of silence as we all stood staring at each other in the living room. I couldn't believe I was standing in the home that just a few days prior, was shared by my husband, his girlfriend and their son. "I don't believe this," Angelica said. "You're his wife?" she asked hesitantly as if the answer would be any different than the one I had just provided her with. "Yes. The better part of my life had been spent devoted to this piece of shit. We even share two beautiful children together, Jessica and Bryson Jr," I informed her while not once taking my eyes off of Bryson. "Oh, so you have a Bryson Jr too, huh?" she asked nonchalantly as though she was asking me if I wanted a glass of water. "What?" I asked her. I turned to Bryson who was now looking like he wanted to run away and hide. "What kind of sick shit is this? You are unbelievable!" I wanted to cry. He walked closer to me. "Don't fucking touch me," I said while putting my hands up in the air. I squeezed my eyes together in hopes that I would open them and find that this had all been a very bad dream. The past couple of days had been a bit too much for me and I just wanted to escape it all. I turned to Angelica, "Please forgive me for coming over unannounced. I just wanted to go over a couple of things with you but it looks like somebody already beat me to it." I rolled my eyes at Bryson so vehemently that I thought they were going to be sealed shut when I tried to reopen them.

She grabbed her purse from the counter immediately. "Yes, of course. How much do I owe you?" she asked in a cracked voice, clearly trying hard to play the macho role and hold herself together. "Angelica, honey, it's on the house," I gave Bryson a nasty stare. He was standing against the wall looking hopeless. "Actually, I should be the one paying you," I said before walking out of the house.

FORTY – SEVEN – BRYSON

The look on my wife's face when she walked into the home that I had shared with Angelica was one that I will never forget. She stared at me with pure hatred while she talked to the woman who she now knew as my mistress. The look on her face was one that you would only give your worst enemy. She despised me and I deserved every bit of the anger she felt towards me. I couldn't help but think about Kyle's advice. I wondered if maybe I should have listened to him and left things the way that they were. At least that way I would have a place to sleep tonight.

"Hey man, what's going on?" I said to my best friend who already sounded like answering the phone for me was a mistake. "Not too much. Remember this is the week that me, Tammy and the kids are going to visit her parents," he paused." I felt like by the way he was talking, Tammy must have been staring him in the face. "What's up with you?" he asked. "Man, if I said everything was going good, I'd be lying," I replied. "She found out, didn't she?" he asked. "Man, I told you all of that shit you were talking was a bad idea from the jump. Now look at your ass," he said. "Listen, Tammy is inside the gas station with the kids and I can't talk but another minute. "I need a favor," I said getting straight to the point. "Like what?" he asked. "Kyle, I don't have anywhere to go. I can't get into it right now but my ass is homeless man," I said. "So what, you need to hold something?" he asked. "Well I was hoping to house sit for a couple of days. Is the key still in the flower pot on the front porch?" I asked. "No can do man. If I do that, I will be homeless along with you when we get back. Tammy and Peyton have been talking and right now, you are on both of their shit lists. I'm sorry but there's nothing I can do man," he said. "Look, Tammy is walking over here fast as hell, like she reading my lips from a mile away. Let me hit you back when we get back into town," he said before abruptly ending the call.

"Information. What's your city and state?" stated the familiar voice on the other end of the phone. "Baltimore, Maryland," I stated. "And what listing," the robot sounding woman asked. "Bluebay Suites," I stated. Hell, I figured if I was going to be homeless until God knows when, I might as well be comfortable at my favorite hotel. It also didn't hurt that the last time Peyton and I had stayed there, we had won two free nights for being the fiftieth guests of the day. "That number is 410-555-5267. Would you like for me to connect you?" she asked.

After being connected, I proceeded to book my home for the next week. Since my suite wasn't ready yet, I took a chance and went home to grab a few necessities, as well as, clothing for the next few days. Since it was about twelve in the afternoon, I knew I had a pretty good chance of doing what I needed to do without running into Peyton or the kids. I wasn't sure if Peyton had told Jessica and Bryson Jr. about me, so I didn't want to risk seeing either one of them. As a father, I always strived to set a good example for my children. I really didn't know at this point what I would eventually say to them when the time came. The thought alone seemed to rip my heart out of my chest.

Getting my things went smoothly. There was one thing that puzzled me, though. As I went to grab my necessities from the bathroom, I noticed Peyton's overnight bad sitting in the corner. It was slightly opened and I noticed a small white envelope sticking out of the top of it. There was a part of me that wanted to get the hell out of there but the other part of me still wondered where she had been the other night. My curiosity was getting the best of me and I began to wonder if this envelope could provide me with the answers. I started to convince myself that it was probably nothing and that I should just open it, read it and then put it back where I had found it. Without giving it another thought, I reached down, grabbed the small envelope and opened it.

"Dear Peyton,

It brought back a lot of good memories seeing you at the party the other night. My only wish is that one day you will realize how much I truly love you. Frankie."

I couldn't believe the words that I had just read. "What the hell?" I said aloud. I wanted to know who this Frankie person was and why the hell was there a card from him in my wife's overnight bag. "She has the nerve to pretend to be holier-than-thou when she's busy fucking around on me," I thought. I couldn't think straight. I grabbed my keys and my bags and ran to my truck.

All I could see was red as I drove about sixty in a forty-five miles per hour zone. I literally saw myself barging into her office on a mission to demand an explanation. My hands begin to shake as I imagined myself shoving the card down her throat. The thoughts of her and this Frankie dude filled my head. I imagined his hands all over her as they had sex the way the two of us used to. I wondered how many times they had been together and which positions they had fucked in.

Once my thoughts started getting the best of me, I felt a tear role down my cheek. The hurt became too much for me to deal with. I decided to pull off the highway to get myself together. I didn't know how to deal with the thought of my wife being touched by another man. I buried my face in my hands and began to sob. There was no doubt that she was hurting just as much as I was. I had caused her the ultimate hurt. Maybe her affair was due to my absence all these years. If I had been home instead of sleeping with another woman, this may have been prevented.

"Oh God, what have I done? Please," I cried hysterically with my head on the steering wheel. All of the anger that I had just felt towards Peyton had turned into sorrow. For the first time since stepping out on her ten years prior, I sincerely felt sorry for the wrong I had done.

FORTY – EIGHT – ANGELICA

"Is it a bad time?" Jeremy asked as soon as I picked up the phone. "It looks like you have company. Maybe I should come by another time," he suggested. Although I was looking forward to his company and the opportunity to have someone else occupy my thoughts besides Bryson, I decided that agreeing with him was probably for the best. I wasn't sure how much longer I was going to be entertaining Bryson and the detective so I cancelled things with Jeremy to be on the safe side.

"I am so sorry about this," I whispered. "You don't have to apologize for anything. Besides, Ayslan kind of filled me in a little bit," he said boldly. I wasn't sure if I was pissed or thankful. Ayslan had saved me from having to explain this rather awkward situation but how did she know I was ready for Jeremy to know all of my business. I should have known better anyway because my baby sister has never been able to hold water. "All you need to say is that it's not a good time. How about this weekend?" he asked. "Okay, this weekend sounds good. I'll call you later," I whispered before hanging up the phone and turning back towards my unwanted guests.

"Did I just hear her right?" I asked myself. The beautiful woman that I had hired to hunt down Bryson's wife was actually Bryson's wife. I thought my ears were playing tricks on me. How could this be? What in the entire world was happening? I wanted to lay down and die but I wouldn't allow myself to lose it in front of the strangers who stood before me. All the years I had spent in this living room, I would have never imagined I would share this space with Bryson and his wife of eighteen years. I felt lost and I didn't know what to believe anymore. I needed an escape from this reality.

"I guess we would start with dinner, I wouldn't want you gnawing at my arm the whole night," he joked. "Very funny," I responded feeling like Jeremy was the drug I had used to numb the pain Bryson had caused me. After my emotionally draining afternoon, I decided to give Jeremy a call. I didn't want to think of him as a rebound, just as someone to past time with as I worked my way through one of the most difficult times of my life. "How do you feel about going to a cookout? It would just be my immediate family, you know, my parents, some of my aunties, uncles, cousins, my sisters, my brother and maybe some friends of the family," he said. "You call that immediate," I said. I paused pretending to think hard about his offer.

I wondered if it was a good time to tell him about Bryson Jr. I wasn't sure if this was going anywhere but I thought he deserved to know up front. "Jeremy, there's something that I need to tell you," I paused. "Go ahead," he said in his northern accent. I was a sucker for a man with an accent. It didn't matter where he was from. They all turned me on. "I have a ten-year-old son. His name is Bryson Jr," I said nervously. "A little dude, huh? Oh he'll fit in very well with my little cousins," he said. His response caught me by surprise. I was speechless. "Hello," he said. "I'm here, I just thought that-," he interrupted. "What? You thought the fact that you had a kid would push me away?" he asked.

"Angelica, I love kids. "Hell, I love them so much that I have two of my own," he informed. "Two little girls. Seven and five," he stated. "Well, I wouldn't have guessed that. Not that you don't seem like the daddy type or anything but you just," I hesitated. "You just seem like such a bachelor with the way you carry yourself," I said.

"And you don't? If the way we looked determined if we could possibly be parents, I couldn't imagine you standing in the kitchen baking cookies for the next PTA meeting either. You probably won't believe that I have custody of my girls because their mother decided that raising them would be too much for her?" he stated. "Wow. I definitely commend you for that," I said. "No praise needed. I do it because I want to and not because I have to. I wake up every day looking forward to seeing the smiles on the faces of the most beautiful women I know," he said. Not to worry though, there is room in my heart for one more woman, that is if you're up for the competition," he laughed while I wanted to cry. This man was so different from what I imagined him to be. He was a good guy and I can't let what happened in my past dictate what will happen in my future. "Count me in," I said with a smile.

"Hey mom!" Bryson shouted as soon as I walked through the door of Ayslan's apartment. "Aunt Ayslan is in the kitchen. She says she's making a nice dinner for me tonight. He held both his hands up in the air to create a quote unquote gesture to let me know that the nice dinner part was Ayslan's words, not his. "Hey Gel. You're early. I thought you had plans," she stated. "Girl, my plans were ruined due to two very unexpected visitors. She looked confused. "Bryson came by. Oh and his wife, who just so happens to be the private investigator I hired, came by, as well," I informed. "You are lying," she said with surprise. "I wish I was. I am still in disbelief. I've been walking around confused ever since they left. He's her problem now, though. I'm not saying that I have fully rid my heart of

Bryson. I mean, he is the father of my child, but I have started the healing process," I said.

"I'm proud of you, sis and I'm always here if you ever need me," she offered. "Well, you can thank your friend Jeremy for being so sweet. Ayslan, I have never met a more selfless man. He truly seems like the perfect gentleman," I said. "Well, just be careful. I remember the last time you said that," she laughed. "No, but really though, I have known Jeremy for about as long as I've known my baby and I couldn't give him a bad review if I wanted to," she said while putting her arm around my waist. "Just follow your heart and let God handle the rest." We shared a smile and embraced each other with a bear hug.

FORTY – NINE – PEYTON

I had the whole day off and after my eventful morning, I just wanted to go home and hide from the world. Before disappearing for the remainder of the day, I decided to stop off to grab lunch. I had my mind set on a double cheeseburger combo from J.J's Burgers, the best drive-in in town. I wanted it smothered with onions, extra pickles and plenty of their famous barbeque sauce. Normally I would keep it low-carb but I couldn't care less about a low-carb anything at the moment.

After placing my order, I sat and waited for what felt like fifteen minutes. "I guess they had to go and catch the cow and pick the potatoes," I said aloud on the verge of calling and asking what the hell was taking them so long. As soon as I found the phone number, a young blonde came strutting towards my car. I purposely waited a few seconds before acknowledging her presence. Just the way she carried herself confirmed my suspicions that my hunger was not at the top of her priority list. I imagined her and some no good skate boarder kid filling each other up while they should have been preparing my food. The thought alone made my stomach turn. It almost ruined my appetite until I rolled my window down and caught the aroma of my soon to be comfort food.

"A large sweet tea, a double cheeseburger and an extra-large fry," she confirmed my order. I knew that she had been literally hot and bothered while waiting in the hot sun for me to roll down my window. I gave it about thirty seconds before acknowledging her presence. This was payback for making me wait forever for my food. Once I was officially satisfied with my work, I reached to retrieve my food from her serving tray. I thanked her in a perky voice that was sure to tell her I was indeed being a smart ass.

Later that night, I woke up on the couch. I must have been really tired because I didn't even remember falling asleep. I was shocked when I saw eight-forty-five displayed on my cell phone screen. "Damn, I slept the whole day away." I sat up and stretched before making my way upstairs to see if there was anyone in the house with me. There was no sign of Jessica or Bryson Jr which probably meant that there was a game tonight. This put me at ease since I still hadn't decided when and how I was going to tell them about their father's double life. They had a lot of respect for their father and the last thing I wanted to do was change that in any way. Ever since she could talk, Jessica had been describing her perfect man to be just like her father. Bryson Jr had goals to follow in his father's footsteps in a lot of ways. Not only did he often speak about wanting to be a good husband and father just like his dad, he recently decided that he wanted to be an attorney. They had literally been best friends since the day Bryson Jr was born. Friends would call him Bryson's shadow because if you saw one, you saw the other. I hated my husband in that moment for what he had done to our family. Because of his selfishness, he went out and screwed another woman and got her pregnant. I wanted to die, matter-of-fact, I wanted to kill the selfish bastard.

I stared at my reflection in the mirror and I didn't like

what I saw. My eyes were puffy from crying myself to sleep and I looked old. I smiled a few times just to see if I still had the potential to look like the woman that I saw in the mirror yesterday. It's amazing how youthful we look and feel when we're happy. A look in the mirror after a day of crying will force you to snap out of some things. I had to get myself together. I was way too pretty for this. I didn't have to look like what I had been through.

After a few affirmations and promises to myself in the mirror, I noticed that some of Bryson's things had been missing. Things like his toothbrush, cologne and mouthwash weren't in their usual place. I pushed the door closed so that I could grab my robe that was hanging on the opposite side. My overnight bag was on the floor. There was a small white envelope sitting on top as if it were neatly placed there for me to see. I picked it up and pulled out the card inside. It was from Frankie.

"Dear Peyton, It brought back a lot of good memories seeing you at the party the other night. My only wish is that one day you will realize how much I truly love you. Frankie."

After all Bryson had done to me, all I could think about was what could possibly be going through his head right now. "Oh my God," I whispered before dropping the envelope to the floor. There was no doubt in my mind that Bryson had found the envelope prior to me finding it. I needed to find him and come clean about my affair. I threw on my shoes and tucked in my blouse to try and make myself look presentable. I splashed water on my face, gargled with some mouthwash and quickly combed my hair with my fingers.

Now that I was ready to go, I needed to find out where I was going. I felt so lost. If my assumptions had been correct, there was no way Bryson would pick up if I had called his cell phone. I sat down for a minute to try and think of where he might go and then it hit me.

"Could you please connect me with my husband Bryson

Hainesworth. I locked myself out of the car and I need for him to bring me the keys. Forgive me for not remembering our room number. It's just been a really long day," I stated innocently. There was a big part of me that wished I had the right hotel while the other part of me wished for the exact opposite. "Sure ma'am. Hold just a second," the front desk clerk said politely.

"Mrs. Hainesworth, your room number is four-twenty-three and I will connect you." Bryson and I had stayed at this hotel recently so choosing the right one was more than just a lucky guess. After I thanked the clueless clerk, I waited for her to transfer me before hanging up the phone. I grabbed my keys and headed back over to Bluebay Suites, for the second time today.

FIFTY – FRANKIE

I wasn't sure of the reason for Bryson to be checking into a hotel looking like he carried the weight of the world on his shoulders but it made me rethink giving up on Peyton. Her answering the phone crying and Bryson booking a hotel for a week could possibly mean that they were on the rocks. I was beginning to think that this could be my big opportunity to convince her that we were meant to be together. I wondered if I should give trying with her one more shot before officially calling it quits. Although it pained me to know that she was going through difficult times, I couldn't help but wonder what the end of her marriage could mean for us. I could be close to living happily ever after with my one and only true love.

Nothing in me wanted to get on that long dark road home but I knew I had to accept that there was nothing here for me. I knew that leaving meant that I would wonder forever what could have been but I had to go. I was done with setting myself up for failure. It was time to accept what I couldn't change and move on, no matter how difficult that might be.

After my last stop, I figured it was about time to get on

the road. I was lucky enough to bust in on a cookout that was thrown by one of my friend's families who had always been like family to me. The women who I referred to as nana, Mama C, as well as a few aunties I also claimed, had my whole backseat filled with aluminum foil wrapped soul food and baked goods that were to die for. The aroma from the dishes had my belly smiling and I couldn't wait to digest so that I could start the refill process. As I sat at the red light just down the street from my childhood home, I thought about Peyton and how much I truly cared for her. No matter how hard I tried to think otherwise, I couldn't deny the fact that there was no me without her. I had left without her one time before but I just couldn't bear the thought of doing it again. I watched the red light turn into a green blur through the tears that now clouded my vision.

Instead of making the left at the light, I made the last minute decision to turn right. I found myself driving without a plan. I wasn't fully aware of what I was doing or where I would eventually end up. Memories of the two of us embracing one another occupied my mind which caused me to not think straight. In that moment, the thought of leaving here without her was too much for me to handle. I had to do something. I had to do what I had come all this way to do.

When I arrived at my destination, I was sweating bullets. I could feel beads of sweat start to run down the middle of my back. My hands were clammy and I had a million thoughts racing through my mind. I was scared as hell. I didn't know what I was thinking but I hoped for an outcome that would be in my favor. This had been a last minute plan but it was the only other option that I had. I had run out of ways to try to get Peyton back.

Even though it wasn't in my character to do something this cruel, I was willing to do whatever it took to be with her. I didn't want her to suffer because of what I was about to do but I hoped that one day she would understand that I had no other choice. Before exiting the car, I closed my eyes and said a quick prayer. I prayed for God's forgiveness, as well as Peyton's. I then stuffed all of the necessary gear into my pants and walked inside.

FIFTY – ONE – BRYSON

"Welcome to Bluebay Suites. Would like for me to take your bags up to your room for you?" A black guy who looked to be in his mid-twenties approached me. He looked way too happy to say that he was at work. "That's alright man, it's only a couple of bags," I said. "I insist, that's what I'm here for," he nagged. "Alright. Thanks," I said. I helped him load my two suit cases onto the cart then I noticed that he was staring at me. "That's all I got," I said trying to figure out what else I could do for this man. "Oh, the room number is four-twenty-three," I informed. "You know we really appreciate tips. I wouldn't bring it up if I was making over two dollars and forty-seven cents an hour. Actually, if it wasn't for nice people like you, I don't know how I would make it home every day," he gave a pitiful look. I looked down at the ashy hand that was stretched out towards me. This was unbelievable. I reached in my pocket and slapped a five-dollar bill into the palm of his hand. "Thank you," he said. I gave him a look of disgust before slamming my trunk door.

As soon as I finished unpacking my luggage I decided to order some dinner. I found a flyer in the bedside drawer that had a list of restaurants in the area. I had a taste for soul food so I went with Jackie's Food for the Soul which was located just a block from my hotel. While I waited, I flipped on the T.V. and browsed the channels for anything interesting. I ended up on the animal channel. It still surprised me that I could watch these shows for hours without losing interest. After only a few minutes in, there was a knock at the door. It was the delivery guy with my dinner.

It took me no time to down the rice, gravy, macaroni and cheese, hamburger steak and cabbage. It was probably the best meal I had in a long time. I swear they had a bunch of older black women in the back making this food from scratch. After washing it down with a grape soda I had gotten from the vending machine, I was more than satisfied. The only thing I wanted to do at this point was lay down and sleep until it was time for me to get up and go to work in the morning. I threw the covers back on the bed and climbed inside.

As I relaxed my body, I also tried to relax my mind. It was a difficult task since all I could think about was my wife and this Frankie motherfucker. I mentally traveled back to the party the other night and tried to remember every dude's face that had been there. I wanted to know who this man was and why he was trying to convince my wife how much he had loved her. I tried to convince myself that he could have been anybody and that finding him could be more like searching for a needle in a haystack. All of a sudden the comfort of the bed got the best of me and my eyes began to feel heavy.

I couldn't have been sleeping for more than twenty minutes when the phone rang and scared the shit out of me. It caught me by surprise since I had told no one that I would be here. "Hello," I said. There was no answer. I dismissed it as the wrong number. I figured it must have been someone who was trying to contact the person who had occupied this room prior to my arrival. I decided not to think too much of it and turned off the T.V. before falling back to sleep.

I must have been dreaming good before I heard a knock at my door. I cracked my eyes open just enough to steal a glance of the bedside clock. It was ten o'clock. I sat up in bed for a few seconds and tried to figure out if this was a dream or indeed reality before I got out of bed and opened the door. Within seconds of the first knock, there was another one that followed. "Who in the hell?" I thought to myself. I made my way over to the door and looked through the peep hole. I saw a beautiful pair of green eyes staring back at me, as if she could see me. I figured she was part of the hotel staff, so I didn't hesitate to open the door.

"Is there something wrong?" I asked sleepily. "Mr. Hainesworth," she said nicely. "I am so sorry to bother you this late at night but I'm making my rounds and I have a few questions to ask you regarding your stay with us. Is it okay if I come in?" she asked innocently. "Can this wait until morning?" I asked. "It could," she said shyly. "But my shift is over at midnight and my boss wants this done tonight. He'll be in first thing in the morning looking for at least twenty completed surveys, sir," she said pitifully. I figured it wouldn't take too long so I opened the door all the way and signaled for her to come inside.

As soon as I closed the door she turned around and hit me in the back with a tire iron. "Ahh shit," I said while hunched over, wondering what in the hell I had done to deserve such a blow. The look in her eyes told me that she definitely had a personal vengeance against me. I knew at that moment that she was not a Bluebay Suites employee. I sat shaking on the floor confused with a million questions running through my mind.

FIFTY – TWO – VICTOR

I grabbed my phone and jumped up from the couch. I couldn't make out exactly what was going on but it was clear that someone was in serious trouble. It sounded like the kind of thing that you would normally witness out on the streets. I didn't know what to do. I started putting on my clothes because I didn't feel comfortable being undressed while listening to the cries that were coming from the room next door. The mayhem was too close for comfort and I didn't know if things would take a turn for the worse.

I spent the next few minutes listening to the sobs that seemed to be coming from a grown ass man. "What the fuck is going on over there?" I whispered to myself. A part of me wanted to intervene but I also wondered if sticking my nose in these people's business was a wise decision or not. I had to think about what I was doing before I got caught up in some shit that didn't have anything to do with me.

Growing up, I learned very quickly that you didn't get involved in anything that had nothing to do with you. I actually saw a man get killed once for trying to help a woman in a park who was having an altercation with her significant other. My wife had grown up totally different. Any time our neighbors would have one of their late night fights outside, she would literally stand at the window with all of the lights off and watch from beginning to end. I didn't know if she found other people's fights entertaining or if she wanted to be a witness in case one of them had gotten the best of the other. You got killed for that kind of thing where I came from. That is why this decision was so hard for me to make. There was no doubt that someone was in trouble, I could hear him begging for his life. At the same time, I didn't have shit to do with this.

Things had indeed taken a turn for the worse. The man's cries were starting to sound more desperate and I could make out the sound of a woman. She was pissed. When I realized that the aggressor was nothing more than an angry woman, I made the decision to go and check things out. I had a history of calming women down so this wouldn't be too much of a challenge for me.

I pushed down on my door handle and entered the long dimly lit hallway. I was a little nervous because I still had no idea what this argument was about. The closer I got to the door the harder my heart seemed to beat. I felt like it was going to jump out of my chest. Once I made it to my neighbor's door I contemplated turning around. I lifted my fist in the air and was preparing to knock when I heard an explosion coming from the other side of the door.

I froze in thin air. I didn't know what to do. I wanted to run but I couldn't get my feet off the ground. They felt heavy, like I was standing in quick sand. After what felt like minutes, the door was snatched open. I was now face-to-face with the woman who had been the cause of all the commotion. The gun was still in her hand which rested by her side. I reacted by throwing my hands in the air to show that I had no intentions of harming her. She had splatters of blood on her shirt and I could tell by her facial expression that she had no remorse for what she had just done. She looked at me as if she had seen a ghost.

"Frankie?" I was in shock and my voice was a little above a whisper. Her eyes were dark and cold as she stared at me without speaking. I now feared for my own life and all I could think about was all that I had done to her and how I would never get the chance to tell her that I was sincerely sorry. To tell her like this would be taken as a way of trying to escape the gun in her hand. I kept my eyes on it as I considered making a run for it.

At this point, it seemed like the only chance I had at survival. "Please baby. You don't have to do this." I said nervously with my hands in the air. Her cold stare from earlier had turned into a devious smile. "Funny how that's the same thing I would say each time you knocked the shit out of me," she said sarcastically. I felt trapped, like I was staring into the face of the woman that would ultimately be the cause of my demise. I had caused her so much pain and she was now in a position to make me pay for it all. A million thoughts raced through my mind. I thought about telling her that I was sorry for all the pain she had to endure and how everything was going to be alright but the look in her eyes told me that she wouldn't give a shit about what I had to say. I decided that begging for my life was the only option that I had at that point so right there on my knees, I pleaded with everything in me.

"Please. Please just listen to me," I cried. She just looked at me with a stone cold face. There was no way to tell what she was thinking. I still had no idea what she was even doing here in the first place and what connection she had to the man that she had just shot or the woman who was trying with everything in her to bring him back to life.

"If you just spare my life I will-." She interrupted before I could finish pleading my case. She now wore a sadistic smile. Without breaking the uncomfortable stare, she shoved the barrel of the gun into my stomach. "Look who's begging now." She pulled the trigger.

I lay on the floor unconscious, praying with everything

in me that someone would hear the shots and get help for all of us. I didn't want to go out like this. I was in some hotel more than two hundred miles away from home and no one even knew that I was here. Then it occurred to me. Paula was the one person who knew exactly where I would be. She had provided me with all of the information I needed to find my wife and she even recommended the hotel that she had stayed in when she was here once on business. I wasn't sure why Paula was so willing to help me find my wife since I wasn't exactly what you would consider a perfect husband. I had made her life a living hell, as well as my wife's, and I was more than thankful that she had decided to put all of that to the side to help me.

I felt like I could die in peace knowing that my murder might be solved. All of a sudden my eyes started to feel heavy. I felt my heart began to slow down to a speed that made my entire body weak and I was starting to struggle to breathe. The area around me grew darker by the second. I took my last breath that day on the floor in the hallway and my last thoughts were for my murder to not be ruled out as some lie that she would more than likely make up.

FIFTY – THREE – BRYSON

My eyes went from hers to the small hole that had the potential to release a flying, fiery bullet that could end my life. All she had to do was pull the trigger and is would be all over for me. "Who is this woman?" I wondered. She was flawless with her perfect body and gorgeous face and she was becoming more familiar to me the more I looked at her. I wondered for a moment if she was someone that I may have done wrong in my past. She could have even been someone who I had passed on the streets. Either way, I was starting feel like we had met prior to this moment.

"Please. Please just take anything you want," I begged. "We can just pretend that you were never here," I said hoping that she would grab my Rolex and maybe a couple of my credit cards and flee the scene.

She laughed hysterically as she teased me with the gun, pretending that she was going to shoot different parts of my body. "I wonder how long it will take for you to die if I were to shoot you right here," she said as she slowly slid the gun from my chest to my lower abdomen.

While she humored herself at my expense, I began to shiver from the terrifying realization that my life was in the hands of a real psychotic maniac. I deeply regretted not sleeping in something other than just my underwear. Now, I sit here exposed trying hard to keep my manhood from spilling out of the thin fabric. She took the gun and continued traveling downward towards my manhood. I jumped at the thought of her going near my family jewels with the cold metal.

"What's the matter, huh? Are we scared?" she asked, emulating the voice of a child. I felt like I was going to shit my boxers when she made her way inside of the opening. I was really starting to hate that damn slit that was made in the front of boxers. What was the purpose for it anyway? Not a damn sole I knew used it. "Please, please don't do this," I begged with my hands in the air. As if she heard nothing, she removed the safety from the three-eighty and released one shiny bullet into the chamber. I then closed my eyes and waited for what I knew was the end of my life.

I heard a knock at the door. At first I thought it was God. I slowly opened my eyes and focused on the crazy bitch that stood before me. I watched as she panicked in fear. There was a second knock which seemed to make her even more uncomfortable. She tucked her gun into the back of her jeans and walked swiftly towards the door. After taking a deep breath, she yanked the door open. I could hear her greeting the visitor and they exchanged words. I took the opportunity to stand up, all the while, holding my hands uncomfortably in the air. I wanted to get a better view of the person who was standing in the doorway, hoping to alert them in some way.

To my surprise, it was Peyton. "Peyton, please. This crazy bitch is trying to kill me," I took a chance and called out. She covered her mouth and smacked the stranger in the face. "You bitch," she shouted. "How could you do something like this?" she asked as she ran in my direction. The stranger was left standing at the door holding her cheek. The woman stared at Peyton as she ran to my rescue. She removed her hand from her cheek and studied it as if checking for blood.

"You're still pretending, huh?" she asked. I wondered what she meant by this but I was too happy to have been alive to worry about what this woman was talking about. "Go to hell Frankie!" Peyton shouted. All of a sudden, my mind went in a million different directions as it raced to try and find a reasonable explanation for the words that had just come out of Peyton's mouth. I stared at Peyton with a look of horror as she gave me a similar look.

"This," I paused for a brief second. "Is Frankie?" I looked at her with confusion. She nodded hesitantly, with a look of embarrassment. "You have been fucking around on me with a woman?" I asked. I cut my eye at the woman who had apparently been fulfilling my wife's needs. She was standing by the door with a look of satisfaction on her face. The look made my blood boil. I didn't know who I wanted to hurt more; Peyton or her girlfriend. "It's not what you think," Peyton stated. "Well, what the hell is it then?" I asked rhetorically. "It seems pretty clear to me," I stated angrily. "This dike wrote you a letter talking about how much in love with you she is. It can't get any clearer than that," I said. Her face held a look of shame. She looked as if she wanted to cry and I couldn't have cared less.

"Peyton you know your heart has never really been with this man, or any man for that matter. You tried to go against our love for each other and look at where it got you; heartbroken and miserable," Frankie said. "Just shut the hell up. Please!" Peyton turned and looked at me nervously. "Please don't listen to this. I love you. Bryson, please!" she shouted. I looked into her eyes and although I wanted to forgive her, all I could imagine was her making love to a woman; a woman who had just tried to kill me. I was so full of resentment and disgust towards the woman I had once loved more than anything in the world.

"How could you, Peyton? How dare you fuck around on

me with this psycho bitch?" I asked. "Don't forget to tell lover boy about our little rendezvous in his bed," she said happily. I became so full of rage that I couldn't even see straight. I grabbed her. "You fucked her in our bed?" I shook my wife with all of the strength I had in me. "You bitch!" I shouted. Before I knew it, I pulled back my fist and hit her in the face. She laid on the floor helpless. I looked up to see Frankie running towards me, aiming her pistol at the center of my body. With one shot, she had finally done what she had come here to do.

I lay breathless on the floor with blood flowing from my chest. I finally knew what people meant when they said their whole life flashes before their eyes when facing death. I had visions of Peyton as she walked down the aisle in her wedding dress, along with instant flashing pictures of my children when they were smaller. I was welcomed back to reality by a choking sound that came from my mouth. From what I had seen in movies, I knew that this couldn't be good.

FIFTY – FOUR – BRYSON

I woke up a couple of days later in the hospital hooked up to all kinds of machines. There were at least ten different tubes coming from just about every part of my body. Everything hurt from my shoulders to the tips of my toes.

I looked around the room and to my surprise, I found Peyton sitting in a recliner by the wall chatting with Angelica. It was a sight that I had not been prepared for and it left me confused.

I scanned the room further and found Jessica and B.J. standing by the window entertaining Bryson Jr. At this point, I was sure that I had indeed died and I was now in heaven or even hell for that matter.

"Bryson," Peyton called out softly from across the room. "Hey," she whispered as she came closer to my bedside. "What's going on," I wasted no time asking. She gave me what I knew very well to be a forced smile. "Do you remember anything?" she asked hesitantly. "The last thing I remember is being asleep at Bluebay Suites. Everything after that is a blur," I responded weakly. She grabbed my hand and pulled it close to her heart. This time, her face contained a sincere, pleasant smile. "Baby, it was a random robbery.

Officer Wilkins said that it's the third time this month that they've hit a hotel on this side of town," she stated before hanging her head low. "You were hit but the doctor says that you will make a full recovery," she finished. Since I hadn't remembered anything, I listened carefully and tried to piece everything together that she was telling me.

I looked up at her and I wasn't sure what had brought about such positive changes. I had gone to sleep with the weight of the world on my shoulders and I had awaken to much better circumstances. It appeared as though she had forgiven me and I couldn't have been more grateful. "Peyton, I am so sorry for all that I have done to you. Baby, if you forgive me, I'll-," she cut me off before I could finish. "Shh," she put her finger to her lips and shook her head. "That's all in the past now. I'm just glad that you're okay. Let's concentrate on getting you better. We have our whole future ahead of us. Let's leave the past in the past. Can we do that?" she asked. "Yes, I can," I replied. "Well, if you're willing, so am I," she stated.

I looked at my children who were standing by the window and wondered if any of them had known about my secret. I observed Jessica as she sat on the floor playing on her laptop. B.J. watched anxiously from the side. It put me at ease when I saw that Bryson Jr sat comfortably with his head resting on Jessica's shoulder. I looked up at Peyton," Do they know about-?" she began nodding before the words fully escaped my mouth. "They know," she informed.

Tears started to form in her eyes. "He's really a bright kid Bryce and he looks just like your mother," she said. "I'm sorry Peyton," I whispered weakly. "No, don't be. It's just going to take some getting used to is all but we can get through this," she said.

I wondered if this was a good time to confront Peyton about the letter I found in the bathroom or not. After all, if we were going to move on together, I needed to know exactly who this Frankie dude was. I looked up and stared into the same beautiful eyes I fell in love with and decided to let it all go. If Peyton could forgive me for a ten-year affair, I could certainly forgive her for her infidelities. After all, she said she's willing to leave the past in the past, if I was willing to do the same.

EPILOGUE

I stood at the end of the aisle waiting for Peyton to make her grand entrance. I thought about the ten years that I had stolen from her. The guilt still weighed heavy on my heart. It had been a year since she discovered the truth about Angelica and I and I still couldn't believe how lucky I was. There's not a day that goes by that I don't apologize for the terrible pain that I've caused her. I still find it hard to believe that a simple tragedy could cause her to forget and forgive me for all of the things that I had done. It almost seemed too easy, but hey, I wasn't complaining. I had gotten my wife back. I just took it for what it was, a blessing from God. She looked so beautiful as she strutted down the aisle in the short cream colored mini that had cost me more than a month's mortgage. A single tear escaped my eye as I thanked God for the miracles that he had performed over the previous year.

I looked over to my right and there stood Peyton's closest friends; Angelica and Tammy. I had been very accepting of the newfound friendship between Angelica and Peyton since we were all connected by the children we all shared. Their friendship only made things easier. To my left stood Kyle, my best friend along with Jeremy, Angelica's fiancé. They were due to be married in the spring of next year. The two of them seemed to be very happy and I was their number one fan. After all, she was a good woman and he seemed to be a good man.

Once my beautiful bride had made her way to my side, I couldn't stop admiring her. She still managed to make my heart skip a beat every time she was near me. The preacher signaled for us to face him before beginning the speech that we had both remembered all too well from many moons ago. As I looked into her eyes, I appreciated the fact that we now had no secrets. This was going to be a new beginning for the both of us and I was more than accepting of that. This time, there was going to be no secrets. We were both free of lies and infidelities and we were ready to start our new life together in an honest relationship.

After what seemed like forever, Reverend Dean asked the question that had caused me to stand with crossed fingers the first time around. Peyton's mother disapproved of our marriage, and during our original ceremony, I stood before the whole congregation sweating and praying that she wouldn't object in front of all of our friends and family. To my surprise, she sat quietly as the preacher proceeded with pronouncing us husband and wife. This time around, my mother-in-law was watching from heaven, so only God knew what her input was. I felt confident that there wasn't anyone else here on earth that disagreed with our reuniting in holy matrimony. "Is there anyone here who has any reason why these two should not marry on this day?" Reverend Dean asked. Peyton and I stared out into the crowd. We held smiles on our faces as we studied our guests. "Well then, by the power that has been invested in me, I now pronounce you husband and wife. You may kiss the bride," he said.

The ceremony was perfect. We walked out of the church to Alicia Keys' "Unbreakable" and I couldn't have chosen a more appropriate song. Once we reached the end of the pews, I noticed a familiar face staring at me. It was a woman whose beauty was so captivating that I almost lost sight of where I was and what I was doing. She seemed to stare right through me with the most mysterious pair of green eyes. Once Peyton caught sight of her, I almost had to push her the remainder of the way out of the church. I whispered in her ear, "Is everything alright?" She gave me a forced smile. "Yes," she replied. I wasn't sure what it was about this woman but seeing her left me feeling uneasy. It was almost like I had seen her before, and by the way Peyton had reacted, I was beginning to think that maybe she had, too.